Angela Sommer-Bodenburg

the little Vampire

IN THE
VALE OF DOOM

Illustrated by Amelie Glienke

Translated by Sarah Gibson

SIMON & SCHUSTER

LONDON • SYDNEY • NEW YORK • TOKYO • SINGAPORE • TORONTO

Copyright © 1986 Rowohlt Taschenbuch Verlag GmbH

First published in Germany in 1986 by
Rowohlt Taschenbuch Verlag GmbH

First published in Great Britain in 1991
by Simon and Schuster Young Books

Photoset in North Wales by
Derek Doyle & Associates, Mold, Clwyd.
Printed and bound in Great Britain by
The Guernsey Press Co. Ltd, Guernsey, Channel Islands.

Simon and Schuster Young Books
Simon and Schuster Ltd
Wolsey House
Wolsey Road
Hemel Hempstead HP2 4SS

British Library Cataloguing in Publication Data
Sommer-Bodenburg, Angela
   Little vampire in the vale of doom, the.
   I. Title II. Series
   823'.914 [J]

ISBN 0 7500 0409 6
ISBN 0 7500 0410 X (Pbk)

Contents

The Inventory   1
The Christmas List   7
A Fine Mess!   10
Another Present   15
Living? If Only I Were!   19
An Unexpected Turn of Events   27
Haunted Holiday?   30
It All Depends on the Person   35
The Vale of Doom   39
Wolf 's Hollow   42
Truth and Fiction   46
Moonlight over the Vale of Doom   50
Like a World Champion   54
The Princess of Darkness   56
A Close Shave   59
A Peculiar Mark   63
The Secret Passage   67
The Vampires' Coffins   71
The Cry   74
The Grim Reaper   79
The *Doom Gazette*   81
The Time Till Darkness   84
True Friendship   86

I Want to Stay as I Am!   92
Fellow Skittlers   96
The Secret   101
Fly, Ball, Fly!   103
Leo the Gallant   107
Never Put off Till Tomorrow   109
A Wet Blanket   113
Guilty Feelings   116
This Could Spell Trouble   120
Firstly, Secondly, Thirdly . . . and Fourthly   123
Now Prick up Your Ears!   127
Till I Die   133
Rudolph the Poet   137

The Characters
in this Book

Tony is a boy who loves reading
horror stories.
His favourite books are
about vampires, and he
knows all about
their habits and the
way they live.

Tony's parents don't really believe
in vampires.

Tony's father works in an office; his mother is a teacher.

Rudolph, the Little Vampire, has
been a vampire for at least
a hundred and fifty years.
He became a vampire
while he was still
a child and that is
why he is so small. His

friendship with Tony began when Tony was all alone in his house yet again. Suddenly, there was the Little Vampire sitting on the windowsill. Tony was terrified, but the Little Vampire reassured him that he had already "eaten". In fact, Tony had imagined vampires would be much more frightening, and after Rudolph had told him how much he, too, loved reading vampire stories, and admitted that he was afraid of the dark, Tony began to get on well with him. From that moment on, Tony's rather boring life became very exciting. The Little Vampire brought him a special cloak, and together they flew to the cemetery and to the Sackville-Bagg family vault. Soon Tony had got to know other members of the vampire family:

Anna is Rudolph's sister – his "little" sister, as he likes to point out. In fact, Anna is nearly as strong as Rudolph, and much braver than he. She likes vampire stories, too.

Gruesome Gregory, Rudolph's elder brother, is a very irritable vampire. His croaky voice goes up and down, which shows he is still an adolescent. The worst of it is he will never grow out of this difficult phase because he became a vampire during puberty.

Aunt Dorothy is the most blood-thirsty vampire of them all. Your life would certainly be in danger if you bumped into her after dark.

Tony has not met the Little Vampire's other relations personally, but he has seen their coffins in the family vault.

The night-watchman of the cemetery, Mr McRookery, is always hunting vampires. That is why the vampires have had to move their coffins from the underground vault to the ruined castle in the Vale of Doom.

Sniveller comes from Watford and is the assistant gardener. His job is to help McRookery keep the cemetery tidy and to hunt down the vampires.

The Inventory

It was 7 December, a grey and dismal day. Tony's mood was equally grey and dismal. He was sitting at his desk with the lamp on, staring at the blank white page in front of him. His mother had suggested he make a list of all the things he wanted for Christmas. It would shake him out of his gloomy mood, she said.

But Tony was not looking forward to Christmas one little bit. The thought of the Christmas tree, sparkling with decorations and with all the presents underneath, even the thought of a cosy Christmas dinner with delicious things to eat and games to play afterwards, only gave him a pain in his stomach.

Anna and Rudolph, his best friends, were probably going to have the worst Christmas of their – um – lives, so Tony could not enjoy the preparations and celebrations.

With a shaky hand, he began to write:

I wish that Anna and Rudolph would come back. I wish they could move back to their old vault. And I wish McRookery and Sniveller could be transferred to a cemetery on the other side of the world!

After he had written that, he began to feel a bit better.

He went over to the cupboard and looked under his pullovers for the ragged old vampire cloak that Anna had let him keep when she left.

"You can keep this," she had said, "so we won't forget each other."

Several weeks had passed since then, and Tony had not seen her even once. It had been on the night that the vampires moved to the Vale of Doom. Anna had been in a great hurry, and had only been able to tell him that everything had gone well and that they would now be living in one of the wings of the ruins there.

There was a knock and Tony lifted his head with a start.

"What is it?" he called grumpily. "I haven't finished the list yet."

But instead of an answer, the knocking started again, and suddenly Tony realized that it was not coming from the door. Someone was tapping at his window, lightly and cautiously.

"Anna!"

Stifling a cry, Tony ran to the window and pulled the curtain so roughly to one side that the vase of dried flowers crashed to the floor.

But the figure outside, dressed in black, was not Anna. On the window ledge sat Rudolph, the Little Vampire, and he was looking at Tony with a friendly grin, which showed his powerful, pointed teeth.

The sight of those needle-sharp teeth, together with the disappointment that it was not Anna after all, left Tony standing rooted to the spot. Meanwhile, the vampire tapped impatiently on the wooden window frame.

"Hey, open up! Or am I supposed to stay out here and freeze?" he called in a muffled voice.

"'Course not!" Tony opened the catch in

embarrassment, and the Little Vampire climbed into the room. There were deep shadows under his eyes, and his lips were thin and pale – truly bloodless!

Tony felt himself shudder. Surely Rudolph hadn't come to . . .

"Don't worry," said the vampire huskily. "I've only come to pick up the cloak."

"The cloak?"

"Aunt Dorothy has decided to draw up an inventory."

"An inventory?"

"Yes. Every five years or so, she gets the idea of counting all our belongings. This time it's only two years since the last one, but she's decided to take another inventory because we had to move."

"And what's she going to count?"

"Everything! Our coffins, our woolly blankets, our pillows, our cloaks, our oilskins, our stockings, our shoes, the family treasure, the candles, the matches . . ."

"Even the matches?" Tony exclaimed indignantly. "She really must be potty to count them!"

"I know!" said the vampire with a sigh. "Anyway, then Aunt Dorothy makes a list of everything, and woe betide if something's missing! At the last inventory Greg couldn't produce his woolly blanket. He had lent it to someone, and he couldn't remember who. Aunt Dorothy gave him no peace until he found it again. In the end he discovered Bertie the Bad-Tempered had it. This time Anna's been as bad as Aunt Dorothy, going on at me all the time," he continued crossly.

"Anna? What do you mean?"

"I had to fly all the way here from the Vale of Doom for her sake – and all because she was fool enough to leave Uncle Theodore's cloak with you!"

"Fool?" Tony protested. "I thought it was very nice of her."

The Little Vampire gave a scornful snort. "I see! Anna gets the credit and I'm the one who has all the work and bother!"

"Why didn't Anna come herself?" asked Tony.

"Do you really want to know?" The vampire grinned.

"Yes."

"All right then: she's busy – professionally."

"Busy professionally?"

"Yes, well . . ." The vampire coughed. "The change-over means she's got things to deal with."

"The change-over to the Vale of Doom?"

"Yes, that too!"

Tony still did not understand what he meant. "What's different now?"

Rudolph looked at him and laughed contemptuously. "Thanks be to Dracula for our food and drink!" he said.

Suddenly Tony understood what sort of change-over had happened to Anna – Anna, who until recently had drunk only milk. He turned ashen.

The Little Vampire looked at him in amusement. "Have you got it now?"

"Y-yes!" Tony stammered.

"Good. Now will you hand over the cloak? Or haven't you got it any more?"

"Sure, I've got it."

On wobbly legs, Tony went over to the cupboard and fetched the cloak. As he touched the rough material, he could not help thinking of Anna and how loving her goodbye to him had been. Must he really part with the cloak?

"Anna said I could keep it," he began hesitantly. "As a pledge that we would see each other again."

4

"Then you'll just have to wait till she comes to visit you," the vampire retorted, clicking his teeth together to make his point.

An ice-cold shudder ran through Tony. "You are mean!" he said crossly.

"No, I'm not, just hungry!" the vampire answered, and snatched the cloak from Tony with one swift movement. Smoothly he climbed up on the windowsill.

"See you, Tony!" he said, and flew away.

Tony rushed to the window. "When?" he called after the vampire, but Rudolph gave no answer. Tony watched him getting smaller and smaller, till finally he was swallowed up by the darkness.

The Christmas List

There was another knock, this time at the bedroom door. Tony just managed to shut the window before his mother came in.

"Well, Tony," she said, with an enquiring glance at his desk, "have you finished your Christmas list?" She stopped and sniffed. "It smells so sour in here," she said.

Tony's face darkened. "Well, I'm feeling sour! You're in here every five minutes wanting something!"

"Have you jotted down anything you want?" she asked, going over to his desk.

"Hey, you can't read that!" Tony cried – but it was too late.

"I wish that Anna and Rudolph would come back," she read, half out loud. "I wish they could move back to their old vault —"

She got no further, for Tony snatched the piece of paper, crumpled it into a ball and stuffed in into his trouser pocket.

Mum looked at him, her eyes wide with astonishment. "That's your list of what you want for Christmas, Tony?" Then she laughed. "No, no, it must be one of your jokes. You're really after all the usual things a boy of your age wants."

7

"That's what you think!" Tony retorted. "Shall I tell you what I'd like?"

She nodded.

"I would like some invisible ink – and at long last a key for my bedroom door!"

For a moment, Tony's mother was speechless. Then she answered coolly, "You know that Dad and I never lock our bedroom door. So you don't need a key, either!"

With that, she whirled out of the room.

"All the usual things a boy of your age wants!" Tony mimicked her. "I've heard that one before!"

He sat down at his desk, picked up a fresh piece of paper, and wrote:

THE CHRISTMAS LIST OF TONY PEASBODY THE FURIOUS

I would like:
   A real vampire cloak
   A set of vampire teeth (from the dentist)
   A pair of black woollen tights that don't itch
   Black bedclothes
   Black candles with candlesticks
   At least ten vampire books
   – and a coffin

He put an exclamation mark after "and a coffin". Then he stood up, well satisfied, and took the list to his parents.

As he had expected, Mum seemed rather upset as she read it. "It's a good thing we've got an appointment with the psychologist tomorrow," she said, throwing an ominous look in Tony's direction.

"What? With the cycleologist?" Tony asked. "Have I got one too?"

His father laughed good-naturedly. "No. Just Mum and me."

"But I'm going to show Mr Crustscrubber this Christmas list of yours in any case," Mum declared.

Tony merely grinned. He was not worried about what the psychologist might say.

"Perhaps Mr Crustscrubber might like to contribute to one of the presents," he remarked. "I've heard coffins are very expensive."

Mum looked at him furiously. "If you go on like this, we won't celebrate Christmas at all this year!"

"Doesn't bother me!" Tony answered. "I'm not in the mood for Christmas this year."

A Fine Mess!

In spite of his mother's threat, the preparations for Christmas went on as they did every year.

Tony's father baked honey biscuits – with absolutely no sugar added, as he kept insisting. Tony's mother fetched the box of Christmas things out of the basement and hung stars, angels and glass balls all over the flat, even in the bathroom. She put a wooden crib scene on top of the lavatory cistern and whenever Tony flushed it, the entire assembly of donkey, sheep and shepherds fell over.

The only strange thing was that his parents never mentioned his Christmas list again, as if there was a plan afoot. Perhaps it was a plan they had hatched with the psychologist . . .

Secretly, Tony regretted not having put down one or two other things on the list. He did need new trainers, and he could do with a new track-suit. And he had seen a fantastic quilted jacket in one shop, and a pair of black jeans with red stitching . . .

But as things stood, there was nothing he could do – just wait to be surprised.

Christmas Day finally arrived. In the morning, as Tony

sat in his room making a Christmas card for his parents, he felt a twinge of anticipation. As he sat painting an angel, giving it tiny, almost invisible vampire teeth, he wondered what sort of presents he would be getting.

Perhaps some vampire books? Or black bedclothes?

At any rate, there wouldn't be a coffin, Tony was sure of that. Even so, he imagined it would be very exciting to lie in a coffin and read vampire books by the light of a candle. There were some very pretty coffins, weren't there? But grown-ups always had a warped view of vampires and coffins and everything to do with them.

In the afternoon, as it began to grow dark, Tony was called into the living-room. Now he was definitely excited, he could feel his heart beating as he went and stood in front of the tree. Underneath lay the packages and parcels, all carefully wrapped so that no one could guess what was inside.

One large parcel looked particularly promising – as though it might well contain a quilted jacket.

Tony started to pull at the ribbon around it expectantly. It was tied much too tightly.

His father interrupted him. "You'd better look in the envelope first."

"I'll read the card afterwards," Tony answered.

"But there's a present in it," said Mum.

"A present?" Happy and surprised, Tony groped for the ordinary-looking white envelope. What sort of present could fit inside? It must be money!

He had never had money from his parents at Christmas before, but perhaps they had changed their minds. And Tony could always do with some money.

But it was a letter that Tony pulled out of the envelope. He read his father's handwriting:

Voucher for a vacation venture – can be exchanged in the spring holidays.

"A voucher?" asked Tony in disbelief, not even attempting to hide his disappointment. "I thought it was money!"

"Money?" Mum gulped indignantly. "We're not the sort of parents who give their children money!"

Tony shot her a dark look. "More's the pity!"

"Do you know what a venture is?" Dad asked.

Tony shook his head. "But I can imagine!" he growled. "Putting on walking shoes and going for rambles – just like we did on that stupid holiday in Nether Bogsbottom."

His father laughed. "A venture has absolutely nothing to do with country rambles. You could say it's short for adventure."

"Adventure?" Tony repeated distrustfully. What sort of adventure did he mean? Probably fishing, bird-watching and star-gazing every night . . .

"A vacation venture is a holiday off the beaten track," Dad explained.

"Deep in the heart of the country, I suppose," said Tony gloomily. That didn't appeal to him either.

"No – well, it could be. By off the beaten track, I mean . . ." Dad hesitated, then continued in an enthusiastic tone of voice, "New experiences, leaving everyday life behind for a while, showing courage in the face of risk."

Tony frowned. "I don't understand a word!"

"You'd better unwrap the parcel," said Mum. "Then you'll see what Dad means."

"So the parcel's got something to do with this – this voucher?" cried Tony bitterly.

His parents simply smiled in reply.

"Well, this is a fine mess!" said Tony, and, with a gloomy face, he began to unwrap the present.

When Tony had removed all the paper and packaging, he realized what sort of adventure was in store. "Camping!" he said, and sighed.

"Aren't you pleased?" asked Dad in astonishment.

"Yes, but —" Tony looked at the presents, undecided. The tent looked pretty roomy, the sleeping bag was soft and padded, and you could use the sheath knife to carve some brilliant things. He could see himself setting out on an exploratory prowl at night with the torch, too.

But to do all this with his parents . . . They were bound to want to have a lie-in every morning, and then they would want to go for walks and have endless conversations.

"I don't think camping is much of an adventure," he grumbled.

"Why not?" Dad wanted to know.

"Probably because there aren't any vampires!" Mum remarked spitefully.

"That's right," Tony replied, just as spitefully. And as he said it, a thought suddenly occurred to him. How would it be to have a camping holiday – in the Vale of Doom?

"Where would you want to go camping?" he asked.

He couldn't believe his ears when his father answered, "We'll let you decide."

"I can really choose the place myself?" he exclaimed.

"Yes. The venture holiday was Mr Crustscrubber's idea," Dad explained. "A sort of treatment to stop you thinking of vampires all the time."

"A treatment? To stop me thinking of vampires all the time?" Tony repeated, giggling to himself. That was

13

really a most brilliant idea of Mr Crustscrubber's!

"I don't see what's so funny about all this!" Mum remarked pointedly.

"Oh," said Tony innocently. "I'm just looking forward to . . . the holiday!"

And that was true. Tony was doubly looking forward to it: a holiday in a tent with a sleeping bag – and even better, of course, a reunion with the vampires!

Another Present

After the traditional Christmas dinner, which at Tony's house was always roast duck à la Peasbody, Tony made off to his room and began to leaf through a new book he had just received. It bore the title *Holidays with Mother Nature*, and, with chapter headings such as "Animal Tracks – Which are Which?", "Fires and How to Light Them" and "Meal Times – What's for Supper?", it did not promise to be very interesting.

Muttering scornfully to himself, "Reading – Make Sure You Get Hold of the Right Book!", Tony made it vanish into his bookshelf.

Then he sat down at his desk, opened his school atlas and, with his heart beating fast, tried to find a map that showed the Vale of Doom.

All of a sudden, he heard a tap at the window.

That was the last thing Tony was expecting. Hastily he stood up, ran to the window and pushed the curtain to one side.

A small figure was sitting outside, but it looked so odd that at first Tony was rigid with shock. Gradually it dawned on him that this person with the peculiar hat and black veil down to its nose must be none other than – Anna! In some confusion, he opened the window and

Anna climbed down into the room – slowly and carefully, which was not how she usually behaved. Tony was afraid. Was she hurt in some way?

But when she stood in front of him, Tony understood the reason: she was wearing new shoes, old-fashioned ankle boots with high heels, and instead of her holey woollen tights she was wearing sheer black silk stockings. That was why she had to be so careful, so that one of her new boots did not drop off.

Now, with a graceful sweep, she pushed back the veil and looked at him smiling. "Good evening, Tony!"

"Hello, Anna!" said Tony, feeling himself blush.

Anna's cheeks had turned red too. "I just had to come," she said. "After all, this is Christmas, the celebration of love." Then, with a worried look at the door, she asked, "Are your parents at home?"

Tony nodded. "Yes. But they're watching television. All the Christmas programmes."

"Oh, I see." She gave a sigh of relief. "I've brought a little present for you."

With that, she pulled from under her cloak a narrow, gift-wrapped package and held it out to Tony.

"But . . . I haven't got anything for you," he said apologetically.

"Oh yes, you have!" she answered. "The fact that I can give you a present and that I can come and visit you – that's present enough for me!"

Tony lowered his eyes in surprise. He had turned very red.

"Aren't you going to open it?" asked Anna softly.

"Uh, yeah." He loosened the paper with quivering fingers.

A small bottle, like a perfume bottle, emerged. The label had been torn off, and a new one, written by hand, had been put in its place. Tony struggled to puzzle out the letters.

"F-r-a-g-r-a-n-c-e o-f E-t-e-r-n-a-l L-o-v-e," he read. "Fragrance of Eternal Love?" he repeated, looking questioningly at Anna.

She nodded, shamefaced. "I concocted it for us," she whispered. "No one else in the whole world will smell of it, just you and me!"

"Smell?" said Tony with justifiable misgiving. The stinging, sick-making pong of the other vampire perfumes was still all too fresh in his memory. "Have you tried it yet?" he asked.

"How could I?" she retorted crossly. "We have to use it together, how, here." Then she added, "It has a very special effect!"

"A very special effect?" Tony had been on the point of unscrewing the top, but now he paused in concern. "Not that I might . . ."

He hesitated to say what his worst suspicion was.

But Anna understood straight away.

"No, of course not!" she said, with mild reproach in her voice. "You could never be turned into a vampire just from a perfume. Not even from Fragrance of Eternal Love," she added with a slight smile of regret. "The effect it has is a different one."

"What happens?" asked Tony, who was still distrustful.

"We'll never feel lonely again," she answered simply. "Now go on, open the bottle!"

17

Living? If Only I Were!

Tony unscrewed the top reluctantly. Secretly, he was prepared to smell something revolting enough to make his stomach heave. So he was all the more surprised when out of the bottle wafted a heavy, rather sweet perfume.

"Do you like Fragrance of Eternal Love?" he heard Anna whisper.

"Yes," he replied in astonishment. "It smells like – like roses!"

Anna giggled. "It's got roses in it – roses from the cemetery. I only collected the petals of red roses, since red is the colour of love."

"The colour of love?" Tony repeated suspiciously. For Rudolph, the colour red had quite a different meaning – blood! He shivered.

Anna seemed to have guessed his thoughts. "You think red only means one thing to us!" she said aggressively. "But it's not true! We aren't all the same, just as you humans aren't all the same. And just so you'll believe it, let me tell you I don't want to be a proper vampire any more."

"You don't? But you've just grown vampire teeth!"

"Oh, is that what you think?"

With a triumphant laugh, she bared her spotless white teeth, and to his utter amazement Tony saw that instead of pointed canine teeth, Anna's were still short and rather stubby.

"How – how can that be?" he said in astonishment. "You said yourself that you were growing vampire teeth. And that you had to suck a dummy so that your teeth would grow long and pointed."

"Don't remind me of that dummy!" she retorted grandly. "I threw it away. If I don't want to turn into a proper vampire, I don't need to grow vampire teeth. What's more, I'm trying to drink milk again," she added, "although it has to be diluted."

"And is it working?"

Anna lifted her chin and made a determined face. "It's just a question of wanting it enough!"

Tony stared at her, speechless.

Then her expression changed and, smiling tenderly at Tony, she said, "And the main thing is, to know who it is you're doing it for."

Tony was so confused that he just did not know what to say.

"I've been thinking it all through carefully," he heard Anna continue. "If you don't want to be a vampire, then I don't want to be a vampire either – at any rate, not a proper one!" She said it as freely and naturally as if it were the simplest matter in the world.

Tony, on the other hand, felt his ears turning redder and redder as he listened. In his embarrassment, he took a few drops of Fragrance of Eternal Love and rubbed them on his hands.

"Oh yes, me too!" Anna exclaimed enthusiastically. "I want to smell just the same way as you do!"

Tony handed her the bottle and she dripped the

perfume on her cloak and the extraordinary, circular hat. The room was filled with an almost unbearably strong scent of roses.

"What have the other vampires got to say about it?" Tony asked in a choked and husky voice.

"Oh, they would think it was a revolting smell!" she answered with a smile. "Even for me it's an – unusual one, if I'm honest."

"No, I didn't mean the perfume," said Tony. "I meant all the business with the dummy and your vampire teeth."

Anna looked at him with a mischievous smile. "They would be furious – if they knew! But I've been cunning enough not to let them notice. For example, Rudolph thinks that I'm clumsy and hopeless at – um – stalking, and that's why I never catch anything. What he doesn't realize is that I don't want to catch anything."

"What about Aunt Dorothy?" asked Tony anxiously. "Hasn't she noticed anything?"

"She wanted to give me lessons, like she did with Olga." Anna giggled. "But I told her I had to manage on my own, with no help. And that in fact is what I'm doing," she added. "It's just that Aunt Dorothy and the others don't know what it is I'm learning to do."

"And – what are you living off?" asked Tony, feeling his heart beat faster.

Anna looked so fragile and delicate, and her face seemed to have grown even thinner and paler than usual.

"Living?" she giggled. "If only I were . . ."

"I mean, what are you eating?" Tony explained hastily.

"Oh, lots of things," she said vaguely. "Are you worried about me?"

Tony gulped. "I was only wondering if I could help in some way."

"You can help me – just by truly believing that I'm going to manage it . . ."

"But I believe that already!"

". . . And for the time being, come and visit me more often, while I'm not feeling as – ahem – energetic as I was before."

"I – I haven't got the vampire cloak any more," Tony objected. "Rudolph took it away."

"I know," said Anna. "But when the inventory is over, he can bring it back to you."

"When is the inventory?"

"On 31 December."

"Bang on New Year's Eve?"

"No vampire is allowed to leave the vault on New Year's Eve."

"Aren't they? But – then you can't let off any fireworks."

"Fireworks?" Anna exclaimed shrilly, her eyes flashing with anger. "Are you talking about those horrible things that hiss and go bang? One of those – those missiles was responsible for Good-natured Gertie's miserable end! It hit her in mid-air, her cloak caught fire, she crashed to the ground and —" Anna gulped — "was burnt to a cinder. Poor Gertie!"

"She was burnt to a cinder?" Tony was shocked. He had always thought New Year's Eve festivities were brilliant fun, and it had never occurred to him that they might be dangerous for vampires. "You do have a tough time," he said sympathetically. "You can't even celebrate New Year's Eve."

But Anna did not seem to be very upset about it.

"It depends how you look at it," she replied. "In any case, I would never have met you if I wasn't . . ."

She left the sentence unfinished, but Tony understood

what she meant. He felt his skin prickle with goose-pimples. Anna's words reminded him that she was – that she had been a vampire for over a hundred years. No, he preferred not to think about that!

"By the way, I'll be coming to the Vale of Doom in the spring holidays," he announced, quickly changing the subject.

"You're coming to the Vale of Doom?" Anna sounded very pleased.

"Yes, with my parents. We'll be camping."

"Camping? Will you be sleeping in one of those little canvas shelters that always look so cosy?"

Tony nodded. "Yes. My parents want to go on a venture holiday,' he explained. "And I'm allowed to choose where we go."

"A venture holiday? What's that?"

"You have to be adventurous, make your own fire, cook your own meals, explore the place – you know."

"That sounds great!" Anna encouraged him. "You can be adventurous after dark and come on a treasure hunt with me."

"A treasure hunt?"

"Yes. I'll hide, and you look for me – since I'm your treasure!" She giggled.

Tony turned away in embarrassment. Why did Anna always have to be so direct?

"There is other treasure, though," he heard her say. "These boots, for instance, and the stockings and hat – I found them all in the cellar. There are things you might like down there, too."

She slipped off the boots and put them under her cloak. Standing there in her stockings, she looked even more fragile and delicate than before, Tony thought.

"The shoes used to belong to one of the ladies of the

castle," she explained. "It's a pity they're a bit too big for me, especially when I'm flying." She climbed lightly up on the windowsill.

"Are you off already?" asked Tony in dismay.

"Off? Well, let's say I'm taking to the air." She smiled and gave a graceful sweep of her ragged old cloak. "Why, would you like me to stay?"

"Yeah . . ."

"That's sweet of you. But I've already spent too long here. Just tell me quickly when you'll be coming to the Vale of Doom."

"When? I'll have to see," Tony answered, sounding a bit uncertain. He rummaged under his books and files. After a short search, he found his diary with the dates of the holiday marked in it.

"Here," he said. "We break up on 20 April."

"On 20 April?" Anna giggled. "It's Aunt Dorothy's Vampire Day on 21 April."

"It would be," Tony exclaimed in horror. "Oh, help!"

Aunt Dorothy's Vampire Day – that was the anniversary of the day she had turned into a vampire.

But Anna reassured him. "There's no need to worry about it," she said. "Aunt Dorothy's quite harmless on her Vampire Day. She puts on her old wedding dress, which is over a hundred and fifty years old now, fastens a gold chain round her neck and lies down in her coffin. Then she spends the whole night thinking of Uncle Theodore and talking to him."

"She talks to Uncle Theodore? But it's years since he . . ." Tony shrank from saying the word "died", and in any case, it did not quite fit Uncle Theodore's tragic end. McRookery, the night-watchman of the cemetery, had run a wooden stake through his heart – eeugh!

"Well, she doesn't talk to him in person," Anna

explained, "more – in spirit." Then, looking at Tony with her huge, glowing eyes, she added, "You see, true love never really comes to an end – never ever!"

Tony felt himself going red – blood red! He turned his face away quickly.

"Keep well, Tony," he heard Anna say. "See you soon."

"Wait!" he called. "When will we meet again – and where?"

"Come to the ruins on 21 April," she answered. "We'll meet in the old, overgrown garden by the clump of hazel bushes – you know, where Aunt Dorothy was hiding on the night of the Vampire Ball." She was about to stretch out her arms under her cloak when another thought occurred to her. "How long do the spring holidays last? Right through till summer?"

"Oh, no. Just two weeks."

"Only two weeks?" For a moment she looked terribly disappointed. Then she smiled once more. "Two weeks are better than nothing," she said firmly, "and it's up to us what we make of them."

And with a last heartfelt look at Tony, she flew away.

What we make of them? thought Tony doubtfully. Anna seemed to have forgotten that his parents would be around too . . .

An Unexpected Turn of Events

Two weeks before the beginning of the spring holidays, Tony's mother suddenly announced that she would rather not come on the venture.

Tony nearly choked, he was so surprised, and he had a frantic coughing fit.

"Why?" he asked eventually, when he had recovered.

As he said it, thoughts went tumbling through his mind. A holiday without his mother would mean that he would be able to move around much more freely and would not have to report on everything he was up to. Above all, he would have much more opportunity of meeting up with Anna and Rudolph, since his father did not believe in vampires.

Tony had to bite his lip so that his mother would not see how delighted he was by this unexpected turn of events.

"Oh," he heard Mum say, "I'm afraid the whole thing would be just too rustic for me."

"Rustic? What does that mean?"

"Well, I do like having a hot shower every morning when I get up, I like my cup of hot coffee, and I sleep better in a bed than in a sleeping bag," she answered, with an embarrassed laugh.

But Tony was over the moon to hear that she did not think much of the simple life.

"Do you think you and Dad will be able to manage without me?" she asked.

"Of course we will!" said Tony. Somehow he must convince her that he would be fine on holiday alone with Dad. "After all, I've got that book you gave me!"

His mother smiled thankfully. "Perhaps it's not such a bad thing if you two go off on your own without me, once in a while. Mr Crustscrubber agreed that it might be very interesting."

"Well, if Mr Crustscrubber thinks so," said Tony craftily, "then it must be true."

He was beginning to find the psychologist a very sympathetic character – at any rate, as long as he did not want to try out any of his methods of treatment on Tony. What was more, since his parents had started to see Mr Crustscrubber regularly once a week, they had become much more understanding and friendly. Sometimes even exciting and surprising things happened – as now.

"What does Dad think about it?" he asked.

"He said we should ask you first, because the holiday was your Christmas present. But if you're happy about it, I think Dad would really rather enjoy going off on holiday alone with you."

Tony smirked secretly to himself. "Me too," he said.

It was a pity he could not tell Anna and Rudolph the news straight away. But he had not seen Anna since Christmas Eve, nor had Rudolph come to bring the cloak back. If Tony had had the vampire cloak, he might have flown to the Vale of Doom by himself, but as it was he would need half a day to get there on his bicycle, perhaps even longer. No, there was nothing for it but to wait for the start of the spring holidays.

Haunted Holiday?

And so at last, the first day of the holidays arrived. Tony's mother cooked them a filling breakfast of bacon and eggs, but Tony was so excited he could hardly eat a thing.

After breakfast, Mum took Tony and his father to the train. "Write to me soon!" she begged.

"Hmm, we'll see," said Tony. "It depends if we find a letter box."

"Or call me."

"Call you?" Tony grinned. "I don't think there's a phone box in the Vale of Doom."

For him, the best thing of all was that for two weeks it would be almost impossible to contact them, and he certainly had not packed any notepaper.

"Of course we'll be in touch," said Dad. "When we get to Doombridge, I'll give you a ring."

Doombridge was where they had to get off; it was the nearest station to the Vale of Doom. But the journey took more than two hours in a slow train, which stopped at practically every station, and Dad forgot his promise to telephone. Tony had no desire to remind him. For him, the holiday had now begun, and he did not much care about anything else. He had only one wish: to reach the

28

Vale of Doom as quickly as possible.

But that seemed easier said than done. They had hardly left the station when Dad came to a standstill in front of a shop window in which books and maps were on display, and announced, "I think I'll just go into this shop and see if they've got a decent map of the area."

"What? Not another one?" Tony protested.

All through the journey, Dad had done nothing but study maps. But of course, Tony's remark did not stop him from going into the shop.

After a few moments, Tony went in as well and pretended to be interested in the books on a shelf near the door. From there he was able to watch as his father paused in front of a cupboard with maps in it, opened the door and began to rummage among the contents. But this sort of self-service was obviously not welcome in the shop.

"May I help you?" asked the skinny, wizened-looking shopkeeper. Everything about him was grey: his hair, his skin and his clothes.

"I – er – I'm looking for a map of the Vale of Doom, a very detailed one."

"The Vale of Doom?" the shopkeeper repeated. His voice sounded as if his nose were blocked. He looked at Tony's father searchingly, especially at his rucksack. "You're not by any chance taking a holiday in the Vale of Doom?"

"That's our plan!" Dad answered.

"It would be better if you did not," the shopkeeper advised.

"Why ever not?"

"Because of – recent goings-on."

"Goings-on? What goings-on?" asked Dad brusquely.

"Well . . ." The man hesitated. "It's to do with the ruins."

Tony could not help giving a low cry, and he clapped his hand over his mouth. Luckily neither of the men had heard him.

"What about the ruins?" asked Dad impatiently.

The shopkeeper did not reply immediately. Tony saw different expressions flit across his grey, wrinkled face. Finally he said, "They're haunted. Even more so now than they were."

Tony's father chuckled in amusement. "Haunted, eh? Well, if that's all . . ."

"You shouldn't take it so lightly!" the shopkeeper warned.

"I'll tell my son about it," Dad answered. "He's mad about anything sinister and creepy."

In the meantime, he appeared to have found the map he was looking for – or perhaps he just wanted to finish the conversation.

"I'll take this one," he said, and put it down on the counter.

But the shopkeeper still had something on his mind. "You – you've got a child with you, you say?" he asked.

"Yes, my son."

"Then be especially careful!" the man whispered.

"Careful?" Tony's father laughed as he counted out the money for the map. "My son and I are off on an adventure holiday, so if it really is haunted, as you say, so much the better!" He picked up the map and strutted out of the shop, right past Tony, who had taken cover behind an umbrella stand.

After his father had gone out, Tony rushed over to the counter where the shopkeeper was standing with a worried expression on his face.

"What sort of goings-on did you mean?" he asked huskily.

"Are you his son?" the man enquired.

"Yes. And I must know what's going on at the ruins."

But before the shopkeeper could answer, the door opened once more and Tony heard his father calling, "Tony, I was looking for you. What are you doing? Come along!"

"I'm on my way," Tony grumbled. He was unhappy that he had not been able to find out what the

31

shopkeeper had meant about the ruins and recent goings-on, but he trotted out of the shop.

Once he was outside, his father said, "I think I know where we can pitch our tent. This map shows a spot called Wolf 's Hollow."

"Wolf 's Hollow?" Tony repeated, startled. He remembered very well what Rudolph had told him on the night of the Vampire Ball: that in the olden days, there really had been wild wolves living in the Vale of Doom. In order to keep nosy parkers well away from the ruins, the vampires had spread the rumour that these wolves were werewolves.

Back then, Tony had felt a pang of anxiety as he listened. Now the same anxiety was back, like an icy hand gripping his heart. He asked with a shiver, "Do you think there are still wolves around nowadays?"

His father grinned. "Who knows? But wolves would be no bad thing on an adventure holiday. Not too many, I mean, just two or three, creeping round our tent at night, howling . . . that would really be exciting!"

He was obviously making fun of Tony – and that helped to clear Tony's head. His father was right. There were still wolves running wild in Siberia or Canada, but not here.

However, his father's words had given Tony an idea – a very good idea . . .

"You're right," he said with a grin. "On an adventure holiday, something should definitely come creeping and howling round our tent!"

And just what Tony had in mind by "something" – that was his secret.

It All Depends on the Person

They walked on further. Low red-brick houses lined the street. Now and then there was the odd little shop, but the whole place seemed to be asleep. It's almost as quiet as the grave, Tony thought.

They met only two other people as they continued down the street: the first was an old man, inching his way forwards painfully with the help of a stick; the second was a young woman pushing a double buggy with two toddlers in it, who looked pale and bleary-eyed. Each passer-by stared at Tony and his father as if they were ghosts.

Even Dad seemed to notice this. "Funny place, this!" he remarked. "Obviously very few strangers ever come here."

"Not in the daytime, at any rate," said Tony, grinning to himself.

But his father of course did not understand the joke. "Come on, let's get a move on," he said. "The sooner we leave Doombridge, the better."

But it took a little while longer before they left the village behind them. Now they were walking down a tarmac country lane so narrow that two cars could not have passed one another. But no car came. During the whole hour and a half that it took them to walk down the lane, not a single car came by.

Amazing! Tony thought, and he started to experience that uneasy, oppressive feeling he had had when they were talking about wolves . . .

"Where abouts is this Wolf 's Hollow?" he asked. "I hope it's not right next to the ruins."

"Don't you like ruins, then?" asked Dad cheerfully. "I'd have thought ruins were just the setting for an exciting, out-of-the-ordinary holiday."

"Yes, of course, but not for camping," said Tony decidedly.

"Why not?"

"Because . . ." Tony thought about how he should reply. It was just not on to admit that he was afraid of the Little Vampire's hungry relations, who had moved to the ruins with Anna and Rudolph. "Because you never know what might be living in them."

"Living in them? Who would do that?"

"Oh – tramps and people."

"Tramps?" Dad repeated doubtfully. "Do you really think a tramp would bed down in a tumbledown old building, two hours from the next village? I don't think anybody would choose it as a home."

No, no *body* would, Tony agreed, but silently. Even the vampires had not moved to the Vale of Doom of their own accord. They had been forced to . . .

Dad interrupted these thoughts. "Don't worry," he said. "Wolf 's Hollow is quite some way away from the ruins. Shall I show you on the map?"

"On the map? No fear! We'll waste even more time!" Tony protested. Then he added, through clenched teeth, "One thing's for sure, we mustn't do so much walking again."

"Are your feet hurting?"

"Not just my feet!"

It seemed to Tony that everything was hurting: his back, his legs and his feet. He would normally long since have refused to go another step.

"If I didn't already have flat feet, I'd be sure to get them on this holiday," he grumbled.

"My feet are sore, too," Dad admitted. "And that's why I'm particularly proud of you. You've managed to walk a long way without complaining."

"Yeah," said Tony. "It just depends on the reason you're doing something – and on the person you're doing it for," he added, thinking of Anna.

Dad, of course, thought Tony was thinking of him, and he gave a pleased smile. "It really was a good idea of Mum's to let us loose together on our own. And we've just about made it," he added, after a glance at the map. "Do you see that bend in the road up ahead? After the bend, there should be a path branching off that'll take us straight to the Vale of Doom."

And so it was. They found the path, and after they had walked through a plantation of fir trees, a broad valley opened out in front of them, dotted with little hills and covered with lush grass and wild flowers.

And over at the far end of the valley stood the ruins.

The Vale of Doom

"Now this really is paradise!" said Tony's father.

"Paradise?" Tony glanced over at the ruins. "I wouldn't be so sure . . ."

"Oh, but it is!" Dad insisted. He had set down his rucksack and was breathing in great lungfuls of air. "To see such an unspoilt stretch of countryside is quite a rarity these days – a real gem."

Tony had to grin in spite of himself. "A germ?"

"No, a gem!" Dad corrected him. "That means something that's rare and precious. As a matter of interest, how did you pick this valley in the first place?"

"Ah . . ." Tony hesitated. "A friend told me about it."

"A friend? Do I know him?"

"No," said Tony, thinking that wasn't a lie. No one could argue that his father actually knew the Little Vampire.

"Well, your friend certainly gave you a good tip," Dad declared. "You might almost call it inside information. Not even the locals seem to realize quite how beautiful it is here. There's just one thing I don't understand," he added after a pause. "I wonder why it's called the Vale of Doom."

"Perhaps because it's doomed not to have people visiting it," Tony suggested.

"That can't be the reason," Dad disagreed. "It may have something to do with that ancient building over there . . . the ruins certainly don't look very inviting."

No, it's true, they do not look very inviting, thought Tony, who had not seen them in daylight before. A long time ago it must have been a large castle, with extensive grounds and a thick wall to protect it. But in the course of time most of the walls had fallen down, all except the tower and main building.

With a beating heart, Tony thought back to the night of the Vampire Ball, when he had danced with Anna in the ballroom to the music of the organ played by Sabina the Sinister.

"It reminds me of the set for a horror film," he heard his father say. "If you were superstitious, it would be quite a frightening place." He gave a self-satisfied laugh. "Even I don't like the look of it – though no one could accuse me of being superstitious."

"Just as well!" said Tony, grinning to himself. If Mum had been there with them, the holiday would probably have come to a rapid end then and there at the sight of the ruins. She was much more sensitive about things that were spooky or sinister – and she had keen powers of observation.

Dad, on the other hand, was once more buried in his map. "We'll be coming to a river any minute now," he explained. "And guess what it's called."

"No idea," growled Tony, who wasn't in the mood for guessing games.

"The Doom! It's called the River Doom," said Dad. "Now we know how this lovely green valley came by the name of the Vale of Doom."

Tony grinned – and kept quiet.

He was certain that the valley had its name for quite a different reason – because of the werewolves, it was rumoured, travellers would meet their doom here.

The path now led downwards into the valley. When they reached the bottom, a little stream came into view. It must have been about half a metre deep.

"Did you say 'river' just now?" asked Tony.

"Yes, well," said Dad, sounding embarrassed. "It looked bigger on the map."

Tony could not stifle a laugh. "Your Wolf 's Hollow is probably a rabbit hole!" he teased.

But there he was wrong.

After they had followed the stream for a little way, they reached Wolf 's Hill – as Dad informed Tony after a glance at the map. Wolf 's Hill was quite a steep climb, overgrown with bushes and brambles.

"Wolf 's Hollow must be somewhere here on this hill," Dad declared.

Tony peered upwards. "I suppose we've got to go hill-climbing, too?" he grumbled.

"Hey, you're not going to throw in the towel at the last few metres, are you?" Dad joked.

"Maybe not the towel," said Tony. "But I've had enough of this rucksack!"

His father laughed, and began to climb. Tony followed him, without enthusiasm.

Wolf's Hollow

They had to climb almost to the top of the hill before they finally came across an opening in the wall of rock.

"That must surely be Wolf's Hollow," said Dad, whispering in spite of himself.

Once more, Tony felt that icy shudder. He scanned the ground in front of the opening cautiously. What if there were wolves' tracks, or tufts of their fur? But there was nothing to see.

"Well, Tony, now you can show me how brave you are!" he heard his father challenge him.

"Brave?" Tony repeated. He was sure that Dad would never send him into a strange cave he had not checked over first, so he answered casually, "Who said I was brave?"

"You're certainly never at a loss for words!"

"Not so far," Tony agreed with a grin.

"Then I suppose I'll have to go in there by myself," Dad said.

He took the torch out of his rucksack and shone it into the opening. Tony could not seek anything because his father was blocking his view.

"What can you see?" he asked urgently.

"Not a lot," Dad replied. "But it does seem to be empty."

Slowly, his father crept into the opening, while Tony waited outside, tingling with anticipation.

"What is it?" he called impatiently, when there was silence from inside. "Have you found something?"

"Yes – bones!" came the reply.

"Bones?" Tony repeated in a trembling voice. "Do – do you mean human bones?"

"No!" Dad's head reappeared in the opening. Tony was relieved to see that he did not seem in the least bit worried. "Chicken bones. I expect other holiday makers have been here before us."

"Holiday makers?" said Tony doubtfully. "What if it was . . . wolves?"

"Wolves?" The corners of Dad's mouth twitched in amusement. "You're dead keen on vampires, but you seem to be scared of wolves."

"You can't compare vampires with wolves," Tony retorted.

"Oh, can't you?" Dad was smiling. "I think they compare very well. Vampires don't exist, and nor do wolves – at least, not here any more."

"That's what you think!" said Tony.

"Yes, that is what I think. Come and have a look in here for yourself."

Tony crept through the opening with mixed feelings. He was amazed to find himself in a little cave which was high enough for him to stand almost upright. It was not as big as the Sackville-Bagg vault, but there was plenty of room for Dad and himself. The beam of torchlight revealed bare walls of rock and a stone floor. Apart from a small pile of tiny bones near the entrance, the cave was completely empty.

"Well, what do you say?" asked Dad, full of pride at his discovery. "Don't you think it's just the place for us?"

"For us?" Tony was startled. "You want to spend the night in a cave?"

"Yes. We'll put our rucksacks across the entrance and then we'll be safe as houses."

"I'm not sure . . ." Tony murmured.

But after considering it for a little while, he thought perhaps it was not such a bad idea after all. The cave gave them total protection on three sides. Out in a tent, on the other hand, someone could easily let down the guy ropes that held it up. And the opening was only fastened with a zip . . .

"Perhaps you're right," he said.

"There's no 'perhaps' about it!" said Dad. He was obviously in a cheerful mood. "This Wolf's Hollow is a stroke of luck for two lonesome travellers like you and me."

"Lonesome travellers?" Tony found it difficult not to laugh. If only Dad knew, they were far from being lonesome here in the Vale of Doom.

The thought of the vampires finally convinced Tony that it would be a good thing not to put up a tent – especially as theirs was bright red.

"There's just one thing I'm not happy about," he said.

"What's that?"

"That my tent has turned out to be useless. You could have given me something else for Christmas – like some more vampire books!"

"Who knows, we might still need the tent," said Dad. "Now, let's go and collect some dry grass and leaves."

"Grass and leaves? Is there some horrible recipe in that book you want to try out? Nettle salad, or buttered dandelion leaves?"

"No. I just thought we could have something warmer than the floor to lie on. April nights are still chilly."

"What about my insulating mat? And my sleeping bag?" Tony exclaimed indignantly. "Are we going to do without them, too?"

"No, of course not. We'll lay them on top," Dad reassured him.

"Just as well Mum didn't come with us,' Tony remarked.

"Why?"

"Well, there's bound to be a horde of spiders and beetles in the grass and leaves."

"Oh, beetles and spiders are dear little creatures," Dad joked.

"Dear little creatures, are they? I'll believe it if you say that when a huge spider crawls over your nose in the night."

"Let's wait and see."

"Yes, let's," said Tony, grinning to himself. He had already made up his mind just where he would put the first spider he found in the cave.

Truth and Fiction

They ate some bread and cheese and shared a bar of chocolate. Then they set about collecting dry grass, twigs, moss and leaves to cover the floor in the back part of the cave.

By the time they had finished, it was already growing dark outside and the air was markedly cooler. Tony now realized how warm and cosy it was in the cave – and how homely it felt, with the candles burning in two little clefts in the rock by the entrance.

"Your idea to use the cave wasn't such a bad one," he admitted. "It's almost as cosy in here as it is in a vault."

His father laughed. "It'll soon be even cosier," he said. "When we've got a little fire flickering outside the cave and a cup of hot tea in our hands."

"What? You're going to make a fire?" Tony cried in alarm. Somehow he would have to put a stop to that. The glow of a fire would immediately give them away to the vampires. And unfortunately the Sackville-Bagg tribe was not made up simply of Rudolph, the Little Vampire, and his sister Anna; there was their unpredictable brother Gregory, their Aunt Dorothy, who seemed to be permanently hungry, not to mention their parents, Frederick the Frightful and Thelma the

Thirsty, and their grandparents, William the Wild and Sabina the Sinister.

"Why on earth shouldn't I make a fire?" asked Dad in amazement.

"Because . . ." Tony hesitated. He must think of something quickly to put his father off. "It said in the book you gave me for Christmas that you have to check out the ground first," he said.

"Check out the ground?" asked Dad doubtfully. "May

I see the book a minute?"

"The book? Um . . ." Tony pretended to search around in his rucksack, although he knew perfectly well that he had absentmindedly "forgotten" to bring *Holidays with Mother Nature* with him. It was still on his bookshelf at home, the one he kept for boring books.

"Here it is," he said with a grin, and handed his father the new book he had bought with his pocket money especially for the holiday.

"*Vampires: Truth and Fiction*," Dad read in surprise. "But —"

"What did you say it was called? *Vampires?*" Tony repeated, forcing himself to keep a straight face. "I must have packed the wrong book."

"Does that mean you've left *Holidays with Mother Nature* at home?"

Tony nodded.

"But I was relying on you to bring that book with you! All those tips and bits of advice . . . we'll be stranded without it."

"Oh," said Tony, "we'll manage. In any case, I did take a look at the book before we left." Take a look – that was just about it! "And I know exactly how to make a fire," he went on. "First, you have to check the ground. If it's not dry, you dig a little hollow. Then you look for stones, but not flints, because they might split in pieces. If the ground is wet, you have to make a firm base first, using sand or something like that."

His father yawned surreptitiously. "All right, then," he agreed, "we'll wait till tomorrow to make our fire." And with an apologetic smile, he added, "To tell you the truth, I'm worn out. What about you?"

"Yes, me too," Tony assured him warmly.

In fact, despite his aching legs and shoulders, he was

46

wide awake – and very impatient to leave the cave and have a look at what was going on around the ruins. But, of course, he would only be able to do that when Dad wasn't around.

"Why don't we lie down and get some sleep?" he suggested. "It's almost dark outside."

"An excellent idea!" Dad agreed, and, as if to underline his words, he yawned again several times.

Tony grinned to himself. He knew from past experience that when Dad was on holiday, he needed even more sleep than usual. This time, Tony would welcome it.

He helped Dad block the entrance to the cave with the rucksacks. Then they blew out the candles and used the light of the torch to creep into their sleeping bags. When Dad switched off the torch, it was pitch black in the cave.

Moonlight over the Vale of Doom

For a while Tony lay there without moving, listening to his father's breathing, which gradually became slower and more regular. Now and then he glanced at the luminous dial of his watch.

After fifteen minutes he whispered into the darkness, "Dad?"

His father muttered something, but did not answer. Now Tony was sure that he was asleep.

Quietly he unzipped his sleeping bag and switched on the torch. With a beating heart he looked over at his father, but Dad's eyes were tightly shut.

Quickly Tony got dressed, pushed the rucksacks to one side and crept outside. Once out, he carefully pulled the rucksacks back in front of the opening.

The moon was shining, and it was so light that Tony switched off his torch. Then he stood still for several minutes gazing out at the Vale of Doom, which was bathed in a strange, silvery light.

Tony could see the ruins quite clearly. They had an even more ghostly look about them in the moonlight.

Just like the night of the Vampire Ball! he thought. And as if the memory of that night had invaded his thoughts, he began to think he could hear organ music coming from the ruins. No, it wasn't his imagination. Someone was playing the organ!

Tony felt himself begin to shake from his chattering teeth to his fingertips. That peculiar, mournful music . . . and the silvery light on the tumbled walls . . .

Suddenly he noticed a dark shadow rise into the air from the top of the tower. It must be a vampire!

There's no reason to be alarmed, Tony tried to reassure himself. After all, he was not afraid of some of the vampires, like Anna, for instance. What did worry him was the unusual behaviour of this one. Instead of hurriedly flying away, it circled the ruins again and again, as if it were spying on something.

On something – or on someone!

That thought sent an icy shock right through him. Supposing it were Aunt Dorothy, and she had already nosed him out!

Tony did not think she could have seen him – the bushes round the cave had protected him. Even so, he ducked down deeper into the leaves, and peered up nervously into the night sky. Several moments passed, which seemed to him an eternity, and nothing happened. Then suddenly the vampire was there, in the sky right above him. Tony felt his heart had stopped altogether.

But the vampire seemed not to have seen him. Without pausing, it flew on and landed on top of Wolf's Hill. Now it was out of Tony's sight. But he could still hear it. Twigs snapped and it coughed.

The cough sounded rough and croaky, and Tony's suspicion that it must be Aunt Dorothy grew. The only thing was – why on earth had she landed on Wolf's Hill? She must have caught scent of him!

He thought of that night in the Sackville-Bagg vault

when he had been hiding in Rudolph's coffin and Aunt Dorothy had called out, "I smell humans!" As it happened, that time she was not able to tell whether the smell was coming from within the vault or outside. And perhaps the same thing was true now: she did not know where the smell of humans was coming from – not yet, anyway.

At any rate, Tony was now positive that the vampire was Aunt Dorothy and that she had caught his scent. In that case, there was only one way out. He must get back into the cave as quickly as he could.

Bending double, he ran over to the entrance, pushed the rucksacks to one side and crept into the darkness.

After he had blocked off the opening with the rucksacks again, he could hardly believe that he had managed to get back to the cave safely, without being discovered by the vampire.

He switched on the torch and peered over at his father. He still seemed to be fast asleep. Tony gave a sigh of relief. Quickly, he took off his shoes and, just as he was, in a thick pullover and jeans, he crawled back into his sleeping bag.

Then he lay there, listening for suspicious noises outside the cave. But there was nothing to hear, except his father's gentle, regular breathing. Tony felt the tension gradually drain out of him, and a heavy tiredness take its place. He switched off the torch, and fell asleep.

Like a World Champion

"Tony, lunchtime!" It was Dad's voice.

"Lunch?" Still befuddled with sleep, Tony peered at his watch. Both hands were pointing to twelve. "Crumbs, is it as late as that?" he exclaimed in surprise.

"Yes!" Dad was laughing. He seemed to be in a good mood. "While you slept, I went into Doombridge, bought some bread rolls and a newspaper, and gave Mum a ring. By the way, that man in the shop with the maps and newspapers stared at me as if I were a ghost." He rubbed his hands together in delight. "It really is the most godforsaken place. Only one of three grocery stores open. The others both had notices on the door saying, 'Closed due to illness'. But at least the garage was in business. I hired a bicycle from them."

"You've hired a bicycle?" said Tony, puzzled. He could not take in so much information all at once – at any rate, not straight after waking up.

"Yes, so we can go shopping every day."

Tony had to grin, in spite of his tiredness. "Shopping? I thought we were on an adventure holiday – you know, gathering leaves and berries, fishing and so on."

"Yes, well . . ." Dad was defensive. "It's not a good thing to make life more difficult than is absolutely necessary. And if I know you, you like freshly baked rolls as much as I do."

"You've bought some rolls!" Tony registered this with delight, hastily climbing out of the sleeping bag.

His father gazed at him in bewilderment. "But you were wearing your pyjamas when we went to sleep. How come you're dressed now?"

Tony cleared his throat. "I – er – had to," he said. "And it was freezing cold outside."

"You've been outside already?"

"When I needed to . . .!"

"Why didn't you wake me up?"

"Wake you up?" Tony grinned. "Do you think I still need help? Anyway, I did try to, but you just wouldn't wake up."

"Really?" Dad laughed in surprise. "Well, yesterday was quite a day, wasn't it? It's no wonder we slept a bit, er, more heavily afterwards. And you've slept like a real world champion!" he added. "Another half-hour, and I would have walked to the ruins without you."

"To the ruins?" Tony was startled.

"Yes! And if you don't get a move on, I'll go and look at them by myself."

"Oh no!" said Tony hastily. "I'll come with you."

It was vital that Dad should not be allowed to go sniffing around in the ruins. He might find the coffins with the vampires asleep inside.

By now, Tony was so nervous that he had trouble finishing off even one roll. Urged on by Dad, he put a second one in his pocket, and they set off.

The Princess of Darkness

The day was sunny and warm, and the air was full of birdsong. Even the ruins don't look so gloomy, Tony thought. They look more like Sleeping Beauty's castle.

That made him think of the time Anna had told him the story of the Sleeping Beauty – her version of it. In Anna's story, the Sleeping Beauty was a young prince, brought back to life by a princess who also happened to be a vampire and gave him a vampire-kiss.

He wondered whether there was an old tower in among the ruins, with a tiny door with a rusty key in the lock. And if Tony turned the key, would he find an old woman inside with a spindle in her hand, sitting and spinning flax?

Hardly! If he did meet a woman in the ruins, it would probably be Aunt Dorothy or Thelma the Thirsty. And they did not need a spindle to draw his blood . . .

Tony shook himself. Luckily it was broad daylight, and the vampires would be asleep. Admittedly not a sleep to last a hundred years, like the Sleeping Beauty's – but they could pose no threat to Tony and his father before it began to get dark. In fact the opposite was true: as long as they lay in their coffins, it was the vampires who were in danger if they were discovered.

By Dad, for instance, who obviously could hardly wait to explore the ruins.

"Why are you walking so fast?" Tony grumbled. His legs were hurting with every step he took.

Dad laughed. "The man in the newsagent's made me really curious about the ruins with all his stories."

"What sort of stories?"

"Well, he said the ruins were a direct link with the underworld."

"With the underworld?"

"Yes. And he said that the creatures of darkness come up from the underworld at night and hold horrible celebrations in the ruins. He talked about gatherings of devils, and flickering lights, and sometimes you can hear ghostly organ music coming from the ruins at night."

"Oh, really?" said Tony, who had difficulty in keeping his voice serious. Creatures of darkness . . . that was a good way of describing vampires! It was also true that they came out at night – but not out of the underworld, out of their coffins. And he had already heard the organ music himself.

"And if anyone dares to go near the ruins at night, he is snatched away down into the underworld," Dad went on. "At least, that's what the man in the shop said."

"And has the man actually seen these – these creatures of darkness himself?" Tony asked.

"No. He said he would never set foot in the Vale of Doom. But apparently they wear black cloaks and their faces are deathly pale."

"Did he tell you anything else?"

"Oh yes. That the Princess of Darkness herself has come up from the underworld to the ruins, and ever since, more and more of the villagers are feeling faint and exhausted." He laughed. "Just think of it! The Princess

55

of Darkness in this grotty old building, among the spiders and beetles and bats!"

Tony grinned. "Perhaps the princess likes bats."

They had almost reached the far end of the valley. Just in front of them, on a slight rise, stood the ruins.

"We had better go back now," murmured Tony, whose heart was suddenly gripped with anxiety once again.

"Go back?" Dad exclaimed, pretending to be cross. "Why, are you scared of the Princess of Darkness?"

"No," Tony growled.

How could he explain to Dad that he suddenly had a feeling that something would happen to them if they tried to unlock the secrets of the ruins?

"Suppose – suppose a stone comes loose. Or a staircase could give way."

"I don't think it'll be as bad as that." Dad seemed unconcerned. "And anyway, I thought we wanted adventure!"

"Well, on your head be it!" Tony answered.

A Close Shave

They arrived at the gate of the castle and found it in surprisingly good condition, even though the outer wall, which must once have been a mighty rampart right round the place, had now almost completely crumbled.

Tony went round the gate and clambered over the fallen stones.

Dad, on the other hand, seemed to find it thrilling to go in through the gate. Tony heard him calling from the inside, "Look here! There's even the old iron portcullis!"

Then came the sound of chains clanging, a screeching noise, and something crashed down.

"Damn it! That was a close shave!" came Dad's voice.

Typical Dad, Tony thought with a grin.

But when he saw Dad emerge from the gate looking pale and shocked, and he saw the heavy iron grating which now was blocking the gateway, his laughter stuck in his throat. The pointed iron bars had shot several centimetres deep into the ground. If Dad had been in the way . . .

"I-I think we really should go b-back," Tony stammered. "That was a warning!"

"A warning?" Dad shook the dust out of his hair. As if he had shaken his fright away at the same time, he said in a light tone, "That was just bad luck. I shouldn't have pulled the rusty old chain." He added cheerily, "Come on now, don't look so miserable! Our adventure's just beginning!"

Tony pressed his lips together and was silent. What could he do? His father was evidently not going to be put off from exploring the ruins – not even by the incident with the portcullis.

They found themselves in an overgrown garden. This was where Tony had been on the night of the Vampire Ball – with Anna. They had wandered into the garden through the giant door of the main building, and Tony had been glad to breathe in the fresh night air after the stink of decay in the Great Hall. Anna had suddenly started to cry – which was lucky! – and had run away from him. And then Tony had heard a muffled voice calling from the garden, "Here I am!" Tony glanced over at the hazel bushes with a shudder. Aunt Dorothy had been lying in wait for him in those bushes, and it was only thanks to Anna's daring and her quick intervention that he had not been turned into a vampire himself that night. And this evening, after sunset, Anna would be waiting for him over by those bushes . . .

"So now we're in the realm of the terrible princess!" his father was saying brightly. "Hmm, well, it is a bit dark and gloomy here, but that's mostly due to the condition of the buildings. When you think these ruins used to be a grand castle with grounds and ramparts, battlements and watchtowers! Now it's all falling to bits —"

At the very moment that he said "falling to bits", a stone came loose from the wall of the main building and fell to the ground.

Tony's blood seemed to curdle in his veins, but Dad

just said lightly. "You see? That's just proof of the sad state this place has fallen into."

"No, it was the second warning!" Tony contradicted him.

Dad laughed. "Tony, you're almost as superstitious as the man in the map shop back in Doombridge. I think we'll have to talk to Mr Crustscrubber about it."

"If you like," said Tony through clenched teeth. "Just so long as we get out of here as quickly as we can."

"Not before I've had a look at the inside of this mysterious place," said Dad, adding, "Besides, I'm interested to see if there really is an organ in the building."

With that, he headed for the main door and twisted the rust-covered handle downwards. The door opened with a low creak.

Dad laughed again. "Well, I'm sure no one else has come through this way for twenty years or more."

If only you knew! Tony thought, and hesitantly he followed his father into the hallway.

A Peculiar Mark

It was a tall room with countless signs of decay. The ceiling was riddled with gaping holes, which let in pools of bright daylight, and the floor was covered with a thick layer of stones and rubble. There had once been a wide, sweeping wooden staircase leading to the upper floors, but now only the bottom few steps remained, and the three doors that led to the inner rooms hung rotten and crooked on their hinges.

"We really ought to leave," Tony urged, "before the whole ceiling caves in."

"Wait!" Dad answered, putting a finger to his mouth. "Can you hear anything?"

"Like what?"

"There ought to be all sorts of scary noises in a ruined castle – gruesome moans and groans, tapping footsteps, the whoosh of a ghost flitting past . . ."

"A ghost?"

"Sssh – not so loud! First of all we must find out if anyone else is here besides us."

"If anyone else is here?" Tony repeated. "Certainly not!"

Not even vampires! he added to himself. Then suddenly he noticed a peculiar mark. It looked as if some broad and heavy object – like a coffin – had been dragged through the hall. And the tracks led straight to the flight of steps down to the cellar.

Surprised and bewildered, Tony followed the tracks with his gaze. Hadn't Anna said that the vampires had found shelter in one of the wings of the castle? Perhaps since then they had moved in here, to the main part of the building?

Whatever the answer, Tony had to make sure that on no account did Dad go down into the cellar. For if they found nine coffins in one place – and Tony knew that the vampires would never split up – even Dad would get suspicious. And Tony did not want to think about what might happen then.

Luckily Dad did not seem to think the tracks were important – or perhaps he just hadn't noticed them. Instead he said jokingly, "Old Mrs Starling ought to see this stairway. Make her realize just how clean our house always is!"

Tony couldn't raise a smile, even though he could not stand Mrs Starling and her craze for cleanliness either. For the moment, his thoughts were busy with the vampires and how he was going to manage to lure his father away from there.

"You – you wanted to look for the organ," he said. "I think I know where it is."

"You do?"

"Yes."

Tony walked determinedly over to the middle one of the three doors because he thought he could remember going through it with Anna on the night of the Vampire Ball.

"How can you be so sure?" he heard Dad ask from behind.

"Oh – I've just got a nose for this sort of thing," he replied.

"A nose?" Dad gave a loud cough. "In this fug, you'd be better off without one!"

Tony's memory served him well. After they had walked a little way, they found themselves in a huge and empty room. Tony studied the floor in concern – it was strewn with bits and pieces, but luckily there was no trace of anything sliding across it, as there had been in the stairwell. He sighed with relief, and went on further. At the other end of the hall they would find the door to the Great Hall.

At the Vampire Ball, a horrible, scarred vampire had lurked in the shadow of this door, eyeing each new arrival suspiciously. Tony could remember only too well how he had shivered with fear under the vampire's piercing gaze. Now no one was keeping watch at the door, and the Great Hall, where a hundred or more vampires had been dancing, looked utterly deserted and abandoned. Of the black shrouds hanging at the window recesses, the lamps with the black candles, and the tables and chairs, not a trace remained.

Only the organ was still up there in the gallery, looking strangely festive with its colourful wood-carvings.

"So there really is an organ!" Dad was amazed, but once he had got over his surprise, he crossed the hall with quick, eager steps to the foot of the gallery.

Tony waited by the door until his father was upstairs and had disappeared behind the organ. Then he left the Great Hall on tiptoe. For he could be sure that for the next half-hour, Dad would have eyes only for the organ! And Tony could use this time to go down into the cellar and see whether the nine vampire coffins really were there.

Once outside the Great Hall, Tony broke into a run. He ran till he reached the stairwell.

Then he moved more slowly and, with a wildly beating heart, began to climb down the stairs that led to the cellar.

The Secret Passage

The stone steps down to the cellar seemed as if they would never end. It grew darker and darker the deeper Tony went. Luckily he had his torch with him. But even with the beam of the torch it was quite dark enough.

Tony felt as if he were deep under the earth, cut off from the rest of the world. And the further he went into this cold and clammy darkness, the more difficult it was to believe that outside it was a sunny spring day.

At long last the steps came to an end and Tony found himself in a narrow passageway which stank of mould and decay. The walls were damp and covered with cobwebs. The floor was wet and slippery. For a moment, he was tempted to turn and go back. But then he moved cautiously forwards, directing the beam of light from his torch at the ground in front of him.

It reminded him of a story he had once read about a man being held prisoner in an underground dungeon. It had been pitch dark, and in the middle there was a deep pit filled with water, just waiting for him to fall in . . .

No, no, there's no such pit in here! Tony told himself.

Suddenly he saw an animal with a long, scaly tail slip out from behind the wall. It looked at him keenly, and its eyes gleamed spookily in the beam of light. Then it

turned round and disappeared into the darkness of the passageway.

Tony was in no doubt that it had been a rat. At first it made him feel quite peculiar. Then he told himself there was no need to panic for, after all, the rat had run away from him.

But where could the rat have appeared from? There must be some sort of little alcove at least, behind that piece of wall jutting out . . .

When Tony reached the spot, he saw an opening in the wall which had been blocked off with stones. A rat could easily have slipped between the stones – and, if a few of them were moved to one side, so could a vampire.

Tony had the feeling that the rat had given him the key to a secret . . .

He put his torch on the ground and began to lift aside the topmost stones. They were much heavier than he had expected, but in the end he managed it. He picked up his torch and shone it into the opening – and there he discovered another passageway.

This one was lower and narrower than the one that led to the cellar. As Tony resolutely made his way down it, he soon realized that he was on the right track. For mixed in with the smell of decay was the sweet and heavy scent of roses – the Fragrance of Eternal Love! He remembered what Anna had said about Fragrance of Eternal Love: it would mean that they never felt lonely again.

And, strangely, it suddenly did feel as if Anna were walking by his side.

Presently he came to a rotten-looking, worm-eaten door. This was where the passage ended.

Tony put the torch in his left hand, took a deep breath – and nearly had a coughing fit. Then, with his right hand, he pushed the doorhandle downwards.

The Vampires' Coffins

The door opened with a terrible creaking noise which set Tony's teeth on edge – but that was all. As he shone the beam of his torch into the darkness, he could see a vaulted cellar which seemed to be full of black coffins. Although he had been expecting something like this, a cold shudder still ran through him.

True, he had seen the vampires' coffins quite often before, but it had always been at night, when the vampires were off flying about . . .

Hesitantly Tony stepped into the room. It smelt disgusting, of damp and decay. He ran the torch beam over the coffins, and was relieved to see that they were all shut. Then he directed the beam over the walls and ceiling. The cobwebs were enough to make your flesh crawl, hanging like veils from the ceiling, and there were nooks and crannies all over the place, where he felt sure there must be flocks of bats hanging. No, it was better not to think about that!

He pointed the torchlight once more towards the coffins, and suddenly went stiff with fear. Instead of nine coffins, there were only eight. One was missing!

Tony counted again: there really were only eight coffins, six large ones and two smaller. The small ones belonged to the vampire children. He breathed a sigh of relief at the thought that everything was all right with Anna and Rudolph. But then which coffin was missing?

Supposing it was Aunt Dorothy's . . .

Tony knew that she was the one who guarded the family treasure, so she might have decided to set her coffin down in a different part of the ruins, somewhere even more difficult to get at. But it might also be Uncle Theodore's . . . Uncle Theodore's empty coffin had covered the opening to the emergency exit, so it was possible the vampires had left it behind in their old vault . . .

As the vampires' coffins all looked practically the same from the outside, there was only one way for Tony to find out. He would have to look inside each of the large coffins. He felt goose-pimples prickle his skin.

Well, nothing can happen to me! he thought, trying to make himself feel a bit braver. He had once before looked into the Little Vampire's coffin during the daytime, while Rudolph was living in the basement of his block of flats. The vampire had just lain like a dead person in the coffin, his eyes glassy and sightless, unable to move a finger.

And that was just what it said in the books Tony had read. During the daytime, vampires fall into a deep, deathlike sleep, and nothing in the world can rouse them out of it. They only wake up when the sun goes down.

And that was the reason that vampires were so at risk. If anyone found them while they were asleep the vampires could not defend themselves or escape. But Tony did not want to do anything to them. He just wanted a little peep inside the coffins . . .

He looked at his watch once more. It was three o'clock in the afternoon, so sunset was not for another couple of hours. Feeling more determined, he put his torch down on the little coffin which he presumed belonged to Rudolph. In the light of its beam, he began to open the large coffin next to it.

It was quite hard work to get the heavy lid to slide to one side. A stink of decay and mothballs hit him in the face. Pooh! Tony began to cough.

He took hold of the torch and shone the beam of light uneasily into the coffin.

The Cry

Before him, nestling in lilac-coloured silk, lay a little old lady with snow-white hair pulled up in an old-fashioned bun. Her skin was shrivelled into folds and wrinkles. Her grey eyes stared straight in front of her and she seemed utterly lifeless. Only her mouth, with its pointed white teeth, was drawn into a slight smile as she slept . . .

This must be Sabina the Sinister, the grandmother of Anna, Rudolph and Gregory, the first member of the Sackville-Bagg family to become a vampire, so Rudolph had told him.

Next to her in the coffin lay a crooked stick, a black bag encrusted with pearls, a pair of black gloves, black silk slippers and a golden book. Tony leant down to read the letters on the worn gold cover.

The Chronicles of the Sackville-Bagg Family, he read, not without difficulty. "Chronicles" – didn't that mean a sort of diary? If that was true, the book must contain some sensational revelations about the vampire clan. Tony was just about to lift the book out of the coffin, when a series of long drawn-out, horrifying screeching noises burst on his ears.

Tony was rooted to the spot in terror.

Gradually it dawned on him that it was the organ. His

71

father had obviously managed to get it going. He began to breathe again. Now he thought the terrible, distorted sounds of organ music were actually quite convenient. As long as they were blaring out, he had no need to worry that Dad might come down here and surprise him.

Tony pulled himself together, then lifted the gold-coloured book carefully out of the coffin. First he checked that Sabina the Sinister was still lying as lifeless as before, then, with fingers quivering with excitement, he opened the book at the first page. The paper was thin and yellowed, covered with lines of closely written handwriting in black ink.

But imagine his disappointment when he found he could not make out one word, not even one letter! Either it was written in code, or it was an ancient script that no one knew any more. So, in the end, he had to put the gold-coloured book back into the coffin without being able to discover any of its secrets. But at least he now knew that there was a family chronicle. When he met Anna later that evening, he would ask her to bring the book with her next time, and read him part of it.

He put the torch back on the little coffin and pulled the lid back over Sabina the Sinister. Then he moved over to the next large coffin.

When he pushed the lid to one side and shone the torch into it, he found himself looking at a tall, skinny woman with wide-open blue eyes which stared fixedly up at nothing.

This must be Thelma the Thirsty!

And she certainly did look thirsty, with her wide mouth and long pointed teeth poking over her lip, glinting ghoulishly in the light of the torch.

She had a long, beaky nose and sharp features, which made her look rather like a bird of prey. Her hands had

73

unusually long fingernails, covered in red nail varnish, and they reminded Tony of claws waiting to pounce. So that was the mother of Anna, Rudolph and Gregory – eeugh! Tony shuddered.

Hastily, he tried to close the heavy lid of the coffin, without noticing that he was still holding the torch. It slipped out of his hand, fell to the floor, and went out.

For a couple of seconds, Tony found himself in total darkness. It was so black that he could not see anything at all.

And there was the smell of decay, which almost seemed to suffocate him in the darkness, and the ghostly sounds coming from the organ . . .

Tony had the feeling he was going to faint. There was a drumming in his ears and his senses reeled.

No, he must fight against it! If he fainted now, the vampires would discover him as soon as they woke up, and then neither Rudolph nor Anna would be able to help him.

Tony pinched his arm till he cried out in pain. But the pain helped him to think more clearly.

He bent down and groped for the torch. There was after all a slight chance that it was not completely broken, and that the batteries had just become disconnected.

As his fingers first made contact with the ice-cold, slippery floor, he started back in disgust. Then he gritted his teeth and felt again. It seemed to take for ever before his fingers touched the metal covering of the torch.

He picked it up and shook it a couple of times – and, as if by a miracle, it lit up again. His relief was so enormous that for a moment he stared at the bright light in confusion and disbelief. Then he headed for the door and pushed down the handle with his left hand. In his right, he gripped the torch – his most precious possession for as long as he was down there.

Slowly and protestingly the heavy door opened, and Tony ran into the little passage beyond. He did not stop until he had reached the bigger and wider cellar passage. His heart was pounding as if it would burst, and he still had the dizzy feeling in his head. But he could not simply run on up the stairs. First he had to fit the stones back into the opening.

Very carefully, he laid the torch on the ground and began to stack the stones back, one on top of the other. They seemed even heavier to lift than they had before.

When at last he had finished, he suddenly remembered to his horror that he had forgotten to pull the coffin lid back properly over Thelma the Thirsty . . .

He felt his hair stand on end at the very idea of having to go back into that pitch-black vault. But if he did not pull the lid back properly, the vampires were bound to get suspicious. On the other hand, they might think that Thelma the Thirsty had sat up in her sleep and shifted the lid herself.

As he stood there hesitating, the organ music suddenly stopped abruptly.

In the silence that followed, Tony heard a cry – a loud cry of pain: "Ow!"

Then came another one. "Oooh!"

It was Dad's voice.

At that, Tony raced away along the damp and slippery passageway and up the stone stairs.

The Grim Reaper

Up in the stairwell, the bright daylight hit him like a blow and he had to screw up his eyes. When he opened them again cautiously, he saw his father coming towards him through the middle door. He was very pale and he was holding his right hand at a funny angle from his body.

"Hey, Dad, what's up?" Tony called in dismay.

"Just a stupid bit of bad luck," said Dad evasively, and began to move the fingers of his right hand, as if to test whether it was broken or not.

"What happened?"

"Oh, one of the pedals that pump air into the organ had jammed, and when I tried to pull it up, my hand got caught and my fingers squashed."

"Squashed?"

Tony studied his father's hand. The middle three fingers were swollen and purple, and the tips were bleeding.

"Ouch! That must hurt a lot."

"It's all right," said Dad. "Don't go and faint on me because of it."

"Me? Faint?" Tony gulped.

"You look like the Grim Reaper himself!" Dad joked.

"White as chalk and drenched in sweat. One might almost think it was your fingers that had been squashed!"

"Oh?" Tony was surprised. In fact, it was not so surprising that he did not look blooming, after what he had been through down in the vault.

"It always amazes me that you can't bear the sight of blood," Dad went on. "After all, you like bloodthirsty stories so much."

"Bloodthirsty stories? I don't know what you're talking about!" said Tony, though he understood perfectly well what his father was hinting at.

"Your vampire stories!"

"Vampire stories aren't necessarily bloodthirsty," Tony answered in a dignified voice. "You ought to read *Vampires: Truth and Fiction*."

"I may be doing more reading than I'd like to in the next few days," said Dad, pressing his lips together. He was obviously in great pain but did not want to let Tony see. He took a tissue out of his trouser pocket with his left hand and wrapped it round his hurt fingers, which by now were even more swollen.

"Come on, let's go back to the hollow. It would probably be best if I lay down for a while."

The Doom Gazette

Back in the cave, Tony's father bathed his fingers with iodine from the first-aid box. As he did so, he screwed up his face as if he had bitten into a lemon.

"I know it'll help!" he said in a husky voice.

Then he lay down on his sleeping bag and asked Tony to read to him from the *Doom Gazette*, which he had bought that morning in Doombridge.

Tony opened the paper without much enthusiasm, for what on earth of interest could there be in the local rag? In the light of his torch, he began to read out random bits and pieces.

"Births, deaths and marriages. The Doombridge Registry Office has registered the following between 26 March and 12 April —"

Tony stopped and read the words again.

" 'Births, deaths and marriages' . . . That sounds if they die before they get married!" he remarked with a grin. Then he went on in a drawling, monotonous voice: " 'Births: Peter Plunder, Doombridge; Evelyn Cattlehide, Doomhaven. Marriages: John William Stubbs to Hermione Hackbull, now at 11 High Street, Doombridge. Deaths: seven.' "

Seven deaths? Tony felt a cold shudder run through him. He looked quickly over at his father and saw to his

relief that he had fallen asleep. He had certainly not heard the bit about the deaths.

Tony went outside the cave and leafed through the paper for further information about so many deaths. Finally, on the last page but one, between an article about a Young Farmer's Club and a report on a black-headed sheep that had given birth to quadruplets, he found a couple of informative columns.

Fresh Vegetables and Liver

The Editor has recently learnt of the death of unemployed ladies' tailor Frederick W., due to spring fatigue, which he had been suffering from for several weeks. More and more people have been complaining of spring fatigue, the characteristic symptoms of which are listlessness, headaches, pale colouring and anaemia. Now the Doombridge Health Office has recommended the following precautions to anyone who is worried about the disease: eat fresh fruit and vegetables, take walks in the fresh air, and sleep with a window open. Liver, too, may be eaten freely and in generous quantities.

Fresh fruit, vegetables and liver? Tony could not help grinning. It was a good thing that the Health Office people did not seem to hold much store by garlic; that would in fact be the only remedy for this form of "spring fatigue" – that and keeping the window shut at night, of course!

He wondered whether it would be better if the newspaper "disappeared". But it was fairly unlikely that his father would actually read it. He would hardly be able to hold it in his squashed fingers. And if he did happen to glance at it, he would certainly not be interested in an article on fresh vegetables and liver!

The Time Till Darkness

Tony spent the rest of the afternoon outside the cave. He ate the last three bread rolls and read a story from his new book. It was about a boy who, even as a baby, showed a remarkable preference for the colour red. From the age of three he refused to sleep anywhere but in the cellar and would only drink beetroot juice, and he bit his teacher's finger the first day he went to school.

The story certainly belonged to the sphere of fiction and not reality, because no one can be born a vampire. But it was very exciting and easy to read – so exciting, in fact, that Tony jumped up with a start when he suddenly realized that the sun had already sunk low in the sky and would soon set.

He peered uneasily over at the ruins. The crumbling walls presented a creepy picture in the rays of the setting sun, just like something out of a nightmare. Was it really a good idea to go over there on his own and wait for Anna among the hazel bushes, as they had arranged?

He felt his heart beat faster.

But hadn't he always been able to rely on Anna until now? Surely she would make certain nothing happened to him tonight either?

Obviously, Tony wanted to wait until it was really

dark. By then, he assumed the vampires would already have flown away – all except Aunt Dorothy, who was celebrating her Vampire Day today, as Anna had told him, and therefore would be completely harmless.

Tony went back into the cave, switched on his torch and looked at his father, who was still fast asleep. Even when Tony sat down on his sleeping bag next to him, opened his book *Vampires: Truth and Fiction* once more and began to read, he still did not wake up.

In order to pass the time until it was dark, Tony read another story: "MacBlood – a Scottish Vampire". When he had finished, he tweaked his father's ear, which was a sure way of waking him up, as Tony well knew.

Dad opened his eyes and asked in a bewildered voice, "What is it?"

"I just wanted to know if you needed anything."

"Whether I need anything?" He shut his eyes again. "No."

"How's your hand?"

"My hand?" Dad gave a deep sigh. "It hurts."

After a pause, he continued, "Be a good chap, Tony, and let me sleep. That's the best thing for me at the moment."

"OK," said Tony, trying not to let on how well this fitted in with his plans. "I'm going outside for a while, to look at the stars," he said.

He was not sure whether his father had understood or not, but he murmured "All right," and Tony was able to creep out of the cave.

Once outside, he waited for a little while.

When all remained quiet in the cave, he set off, quivering inside with excitement, down the path that led into the Vale of Doom.

True Friendship

It was the same path he had taken that afternoon with his father: down the slope, across the stream and along the broad valley floor dotted with little hills. But everything looked strange and different now in the moonlight. The trees seemed like giant ghostly figures, and he had to watch out all the time to make sure he did not trip over roots or fallen branches, or slide on fragments of rock.

Once or twice he was tempted to switch on his torch. But he did not, mostly for fear of being discovered. It was vital that no suspicious noises or beam of torchlight should give him away to the vampires, who might well still be in the neighbourhood.

When Tony had climbed the mound that led to the ruins, and saw in front of him the main gate with its fearsome portcullis, he had to stop for breath. He was sure his heart was going to burst from excitement and exertion. He stood quite still in the shadow of a tree and looked over at the ruins. If he had not known that Anna was waiting for him . . . Just as he was thinking of her, someone suddenly tapped him on the shoulder from behind.

Tony spun round as if struck by lightning – and found

himself looking into the deathly pale face of the Little
Vampire.

"R-Rudolph?" he stammered.

"It's very brave of you to come here," the Little
Vampire announced. "You could almost say you're dicing
with death."

"I . . ." Tony struggled for words. He was so shaken
he could hardly think straight. "I wanted . . . I was going
to . . ."

"You can just thank your lucky stars you ran into me,"
said the vampire in a croaky voice, "and not my
grandmother!"

"Sabina the Si-Sinister?" Tony stuttered.

"Or my grandfather, William the Wild!" the vampire
growled.

"But I thought they would have flown off long ago,"
Tony murmured.

"Flown off?" Rudolph looked at Tony with glowing
eyes. "Can you imagine what happened when we all
woke up this evening?"

"No – what?"

"My mother was beside herself! And Aunt Dorothy
had a heart attack."

"A heart attack?"

"Yes! And if Anna hadn't taken all the blame herself,
then . . . then your last hour would probably have
come."

"My . . . last hour?" Tony repeated, trembling.

"Indeed! It was you, wasn't it, who came snooping
round in our new vault?"

"Y-Yes," Tony whispered.

"Aha! How could you be so stupid as to leave my
mother's coffin half open? You know a vampire can't
move even a little finger when they're asleep. So my

family immediately suspected that a human must have been in the vault."

Tony's hair stood on end. "And?" he asked fearfully.

"They wanted to search the whole of the Vale of Doom for whoever it was. And if Anna hadn't said that she had moved the lid . . ."

"Anna said that?"

"Yes. She pretended she had had a dream that McRookery the night-watchman had arrived in the Vale of Doom. He had spread a huge black net over the main tower, and had caught our mother, Thelma the Thirsty, in it. When she woke up from this terrible dream, she said, she ran over to Mother's coffin in fright, to see whether she was still in it. When she saw Mother, she was so relieved that she forgot to close the lid properly."

Exhausted from such a long speech, the vampire fell silent.

"Woke up?" asked Tony in amazement. "Do vampires wake up?"

"Not normally," Rudolph answered. "But Anna admitted that she was still drinking milk – eeugh! And so she still isn't a proper, fully developed vampire. But, of course, she got into terrible trouble," he added. "And she deserved it!"

"She got into trouble?" Tony repeated anxiously.

"Of course she did! My grandmother said it was a disgrace to the family, the length of time it's taking her to grow up."

"Poor Anna," said Tony softly, thinking that she had only done it all for him. It was for his sake that she did not want to become a proper vampire – and it was to protect him that she had pretended she had moved the lid of the coffin . . .

"Why do you say 'Poor Anna'?" Rudolph snorted.

"You don't care about me, do you? I needn't have bothered to come and find you."

"No! I mean yes!" said Tony hastily. "It – it was very nice of you to bother."

"Nice?" said the vampire furiously. "If it was only 'nice' I've got better things to do."

"No, it was fantastic of you, I . . ." Tony searched for the right words which would pacify the enraged vampire. "I think it was – real friendship!"

That seemed to please the vampire. A satisfied smile spread over his face. "That's more like it!" he said, sounding flattered. He added, with a grin, "But you're right to feel sorry for Anna. As a punishment for her carelessness, she has to stay all night by Aunt Dorothy's side, playing at being her nurse."

"Her nurse? Is Aunt Dorothy as bad as all that?"

"Oh no. After all, she is already – ahem – dead. Probably she just wants company tonight, on her Vampire Day. I bet Anna will have to spend the whole night listening to stories about Uncle Theodore."

"Then she didn't have a real heart attack?"

"Who knows?" Rudolph grinned broadly. "Perhaps it was just high blood pressure."

"High blood pressure?"

The Little Vampire gave a grating laugh. "Well, you know Aunt Dorothy!"

"I do not know Aunt Dorothy!" Tony exclaimed.

"Sssh!" the Little Vampire warned him. He came up close to Tony and laid a skinny, ice-cold finger on his lips. "Or do you want my mother to hear you? Or my grandmother?"

"N-no!" Tony stuttered.

"Well, then!" The vampire made a happy face. "Let's go to where you're staying. Then we can talk in peace."

"To where I'm staying?"

"Yes, to that sweet little canvas home Anna has told me about. I bet your parents are out, dancing or at the cinema."

"No! I . . . we're staying in a cave, and Dad is ill . . ."

"Ill?" The vampire frowned darkly. "So we can't go to your place?"

Tony shook his head.

"That's the limit!" the vampire grumbled. "First I've had to miss most of my Men's Club all because of you, and now I'm not even going to get to see your little canvas house."

"Men's Club?" asked Tony in surprise. "I didn't know you belonged to a Men's Club."

The Little Vampire raised his chin proudly. "Yes," he said, apparently feeling very superior.

"What do you do in this club?" Tony wanted to know.

"What do we do?" The Little Vampire lifted his matted fringe away from his eyes with a careless flick of his hand. "Well, tonight, for instance, there was a game of skittles."

"Skittles?" Tony could not believe his ears.

"Yes, skittles!" said the vampire loftily. "And I bet you haven't the faintest idea how to play skittles."

"That's what you think!" said Tony sharply. "Actually, I've often played."

"Have you really?" The vampire's voice suddenly sounded quite different. "Then perhaps you can teach me a couple of tricks?"

"Tricks?"

"Yes. So that I can win occasionally – instead of always Greg or George the Boisterous!"

"Are they in the Men's Club, too?"

"'Course! George founded it. And Greg has moved in

with him, so that they'll have more time to talk about the Men's Club."

Tony pricked up his ears. "Greg's not living in the ruins any more?"

"No. He moved out four weeks ago."

"Ah, so that explains it," Tony murmured. Now he knew it was Greg's coffin that was missing.

"If you're so good at playing skittles, why don't you come with me?" The Little Vampire interrupted his thoughts.

"Come with you? Where to?" asked Tony.

The vampire laughed huskily. "To the pub over at Doombury!" he replied, and, to Tony's amazement, he pulled out from under his smelly old cloak a second one. "Here, have this! You can keep it – till the next inventory."

And when Tony did not put the cloak on at once, he exclaimed impatiently, "What's the matter? Put it on! Then you can give me some pointers on the way."

I Want to Stay as I Am!

Tony still hesitated. "I don't know if it's a good idea."

"Why not?" the vampire cried irritably. "Do you want to keep all your tricks to yourself?"

"No. It's just because of George the Boisterous. I don't know how he is – um, I mean, what he feels about humans."

The Little Vampire grinned. "Oh – he's very keen on them!"

Tony felt a shudder go down his spine. But then he told himself that Rudolph was probably only trying to frighten him. "You know very well that I don't want to become a vampire," he declared. "And I don't want to be bitten either, not by you, not by Anna and not by George the Boisterous. I want to stay as I am!" he added.

"OK, OK," said the vampire, laughing as if he had made a good joke. "Do you really think I would let George the Boisterous loose on my best friend? No, no, there's no need to worry. You can wait outside in front of the skittle hall, just in case I need a tip!"

"Wait outside?" said Tony indignantly. "That's a bit much!"

The Little Vampire giggled. "Saves you being much bit! Anyway, it's true friendship. So come on, put the cloak

on! Otherwise the skittle evening will be over before we get there."

Reluctantly, Tony fastened the cloak around him, tried a couple of cautious arm movements and began to hover. He moved his arms more firmly – and flew!

He felt his stomach turn over, and if it had not been for the thought of Greg and George the Boisterous, he would have laughed out loud with delight. But as it was, he bit his lip and flew off behind Rudolph with his heart heavy with worry.

At first, it looked as though the Little Vampire was

following the same lane that Tony and his father had walked down to reach the Vale of Doom. But then, where the road bent right to Doombridge, he swept off to the left. Now they were flying over a large, dark expanse of forest.

"Is it much further?" Tony asked anxiously.

"Are you tired already?" asked the vampire with a grin.

"Oh no!"

"I would have been surprised," said Rudolph. "You can fly almost like a real vampire now. But then, you're almost one of the family!" he added. "I bet you only came to the new vault because you wanted to get a glimpse of your – hee! hee! – mother-in-law."

"Very funny," Tony growled.

"Well, why else would you have come?" the vampire challenged him. It seemed to annoy him that Tony wasn't laughing at his joke.

"Why?" Tony repeated, to gain time. He did not want to admit that he had been worried about Anna and Rudolph. "Because I wanted my books back," he said.

"Your books?" said the vampire, startled. For a moment, he looked embarrassed. Then he snorted. "You're the most selfish person I've ever met! We vampires have to leave our cemetery, find a new place to live, and a new – ahem – sphere of activity, and you can only think of books."

Tony grinned to himself and kept quiet.

After they had flown silently for a while, Tony remarked, "Well, I did see one book."

"So?" The vampire was not interested.

"It looked ancient, and had a golden cover, and it was called *The Chronicles of the Sackville-Bagg Family*."

"What?" exclaimed the vampire. "You found our family chronicles?"

91

"Yes. But I couldn't read them. It's in code, isn't it?"

"Code? Well, that depends . . . It's writing that only vampires can read."

"Only – vampires?"

"Of course! You'll be able to read it when you turn into a vampire yourself."

"I – I don't want to be able to read it," Tony said hastily.

"Don't you?" said the vampire softly. "Don't you want to know how it all started, back in Transylvania?"

"Yes, but —"

"There you are! And it's all in the family chronicles."

"But you could read some of it to me," Tony suggested. "Especially the story about you, that would be the most interesting."

"Do you think so?" The vampire sounded flattered. "More interesting than Anna's?"

"Yes!"

"All right then!" said the vampire good-naturedly. "I'll see what I can do." Then he added in his normal vampire voice, "Get ready! We're there."

Fellow Skittlers

Tony looked down in surprise and could just make out a dark building. It stood among tall trees and had a long, low extension at one end. The skittle alley must be in there, Tony thought, feeling his skin prickle with goose-pimples.

They landed in front of the building, which had a neglected and deserted look about it. There was no glass in any of the windows, and the door lay in pieces near the entrance. The darkened openings yawned at them spookily. Tony could now see that the only light came from the long extension built on to the right of the house.

"Cosy here, isn't it?" said the Little Vampire.

Just at that moment there came an ear-splitting crash which made Tony shake from head to toe.

Then someone shouted, "Damn and blast, missed again!" and a second voice responded with a boom of gloating laughter. The Little Vampire joined in.

"Heh, heh!" he giggled. "Greg's missed again. Now I'll win! It's going to be my lucky night!" He gave Tony a painful dig in the ribs with the point of his elbow and hissed, "Now, tell me one or two of your tips!"

"My – tips?" Tony mumbled. "I – er – I'd have to see

the skittle alley first, and the skittles . . ."

"All right! Creep over there and take a look through the window. I'll go in and show you how I play."

With that, the Little Vampire disappeared into the house, and Tony crept forwards on tiptoe. Luckily, there was a thick bush in front of the first window, which Tony was able to hide behind. He carefully pushed the branches to one side and peered nervously into the candle-lit interior of the skittle hall.

At first all he could see was a bare wall. But then a powerfully built figure in a black cloak moved into his line of vision. It was a bald-headed vampire holding a large ball in his right hand: it was George the Boisterous!

Tony had never seen him so close before, and he was shocked at how hideous he was. He had a squashed-up nose like a boxer, bulging lips, and a jutting, brutish-looking chin. I certainly would not like to meet him on a dark night! Tony thought, as a cold shiver ran down his spine.

What happened next was so funny that Tony found it difficult to keep quiet. George the Boisterous went down on one knee and bent his right arm with the large ball behind him, to get a good swing. In fact – and here Tony had to bite his lip so as not to laugh out loud – he was in exactly the right position for putting the shot, but hardly the right one for bowling at skittles.

Then George began to count. "Ready, steady, go!"

At the word "go", he hurled the ball. Once more a fearful crash followed which sounded as though the whole skittle hall might cave in. And well it might, when Tony thought how strong a vampire was . . .

After the crash came an angry outburst. "Botheration! Only one down!"

Tony giggled softly. To hit only one out of nine

skittles was something of a record.

At this point Greg pushed past George, presumably to go and fetch the ball. For a while Tony could only see the dirty white wall of the skittle hall until Greg came back into view. He was holding the ball in his broad, hairy hand. Tony noticed with a shudder that his long fingernails were filed into sharp points.

But it seemed that Greg did not have the slightest idea how to play skittles, either. Looking as if he were about to play volleyball, he raised his left hand and threw the ball as hard as he could. Tony heard a clattering, then Greg shouted out, beside himself with glee, "Two! I got two!"

"Only two?" came a husky voice, and now Tony could see the Little Vampire. "I'll get three!"

"You?" said Greg, with a scornful laugh.

"Yes. Why not?" Rudolph retorted.

He disappeared to the front of the hall, and came back holding the ball.

"Look out, you're in the way!" he said to Greg and George the Boisterous.

Unwillingly they stood aside.

"You seem very sure of yourself today, little brother!" Greg growled.

Rudolph grinned and raised both arms. Now he was holding the ball above his head, as if he were going to throw it in a game of football!

Not like that! Tony almost shouted to him – and at the last moment, he clapped his hand over his mouth in fright. He watched helplessly as the Little Vampire flung the ball at the ground. There was an even louder clatter and crash than there had been when Greg threw it, and the skittle hall seemed to quake to its very foundations.

"You stupid nitwit!" he heard Greg screech. "Now there's another hole in the lane."

"And he hasn't even hit any, either," George the Boisterous added, giggling spitefully.

Rudolph's face had turned a dark red. "Huh, just you wait!" he yelled furiously. "I'll go and run round the building a couple of times, and when I come back you'll get the surprise of your lives."

"The surprise of our lives, will we?" George the Boisterous answered with a laugh. "Hey, Roo, I just can't wait!"

Roo? Tony could not but smile.

"Yes, you jolly well will!" the Little Vampire retorted, and with his head held high he left the skittle hall.

The Secret

Tony peered over at the pub entrance and could soon make out a little figure coming swiftly and almost noiselessly towards him. It was Rudolph.

The vampire stopped in front of him. In an even ruder voice than normal, he hissed at Tony, "Well, have you seen all you wanted to see?"

"I . . ." Tony began. It was most important that he did not let Rudolph see how comic he had found the whole performance. And the thing that must be annoying Rudolph the most was that Tony had seen his defeat. Surely that was the only reason he had spoken so roughly.

So, because Tony did not want to upset him even further, he said, "I think I know what you're all doing wrong."

The Little Vampire pricked up his ears. "All of us? Greg and George as well?"

Tony nodded. "Yes, all three of you."

"All three . . ." the vampire repeated, clicking his teeth. He glanced into the hall, where Greg and George the Boisterous had put their heads together and were muttering to one another. "So Greg and George are doing it wrong too . . ." he said softly, almost to himself, and a broad grin spread across his face, as if he had suddenly had an idea.

"If we're all doing it wrong, but if you tell only me what it is," he said excitedly, "then only I will be the winner! Won't I?" he asked, seeming confused from all this thinking.

"Yes, of course," Tony reassured him.

"Well, what is it? What are we doing wrong?" The Little Vampire's voice almost faltered.

Tony grinned. "You shouldn't throw the ball, or hurl it away from you. You have to . . ." Here he paused meaningfully, before revealing in a whisper the secret – which of course was no secret at all. "Roll the ball!"

"Roll it?" said the vampire, his eyes wide in disbelief. Then the corners of his mouth began to twitch and, barely able to contain his excitement, he cried, "But that's just the way I've always wanted to do it! But George the Boisterous, that know-it-all, always has to know better. He said the name 'skittles' comes from 'whistles', and so you have to make the ball whistle through the air. Huh, how stupid can you get? Just wait till I show them!"

He turned on his heel and, without taking any further notice of Tony, ran back into the pub.

Fly, Ball, Fly!

A moment later, the Little Vampire appeared in the skittle hall with a triumphant grin as if he were already the winner.

"Hey, look, your little brother's back already!" said George the Boisterous.

"Where?" said Greg, looking up at the ceiling.

"There, in front of you!" George answered, giving Greg a playful shove.

"Oh, so he is." Greg sounded surprised. "He looks quite worn out, poor lad. Was the run as exhausting as all that?"

The Little Vampire pretended not to hear Greg's remarks. "Shall we have another round?" he asked.

"Another one?" George the Boisterous exchanged an amused look with Greg. "Well, all right then, one last one – since it's you. But I'll go first!" he added.

Tony found it hard to keep from laughing as he watched George the Boisterous once more take up his position like a shot-putter. This time, he bent his knees even more and hurled the ball into the air with a loud "Uh-aaah!"

But it was all in vain. There was a crash, and then a furious rumble of disappointment from George the

Boisterous, indicating that he had once again made a bad throw.

Now it was Greg's turn. His face took on a serious look of concentration as he balanced the ball in his left hand, holding it high above his shoulder. Before he threw, he said:

"Fly, ball, fly – good and true!
Make me the winner as you do!"

But that did not help much either. There was another terrible crash, then Tony heard him swear and exclaim, "What? Only one? That can't be true!"

"Oh yes, it is!" The Little Vampire giggled. "And what's more, you're about to see the Skittle Player of the Year in action!" With that, he crouched down, put the ball on the ground, and with a hefty shove, sent it rolling away from him.

Tony almost bit his tongue in an effort not to laugh. The Little Vampire had not looked very professional crouching there like a frog, pushing the ball into motion.

And that was why it was even more astonishing to see what happened next. For a moment, there was a sort of rumbling sound, as the ball rolled away over the bumpy, pitted floor. Then there were several rattles and Rudolph gave a shriek of delight.

"Six, six, six!" he shouted jubilantly.

Even Tony's heart gave a little leap of excitement and joy.

"Six in one go!" the Little Vampire cried, hopping from one foot to the other. "That makes me the winner!"

"The winner?" said George the Boisterous in a contemptuous tone. "The winner at marbles, perhaps – you roll the ball for that. But 'skittles' comes from 'whistles', you ought to know that by now, and you can only win at skittles if the ball has whistled through the air."

"Exactly!" Greg agreed.

"But that isn't true!" the Little Vampire retorted angrily. "You have to roll the ball!"

"Roll it?" George the Boisterous repeated, laughing scornfully. "And how do you know that all of a sudden, you Roll-Mop, you!"

"I just do!" said the Little Vampire, seeming, to Tony's amazement, not to be put out at all. He supposed it was because the Little Vampire was right, and he had won! "And in any case, we agreed that you were allowed to throw the ball how you liked," Rudolph added firmly.

"Agreed, agreed," George the Boisterous mimicked. Apparently he could not think of anything better to say. "Come on, let's go," he said to Greg.

"Yeah, let's go," Greg agreed. "The game's not being played properly here."

"You're the ones who aren't playing the game!" the Little Vampire exclaimed. "You can't bear to lose!"

"Us?" said George the Boisterous and Greg together, looking at each other and pretending to be indignant.

"Your little brother is so highly strung today," George the Boisterous remarked. "He's a real bag of nerves."

They grinned and turned to go.

"It's you two who are bags!" Rudolph called after them. "You're real bag leaders, and spoilsports!"

"Bag leaders – how sweet!" Tony heard George the Boisterous giggle. "Greg, I hearby proclaim you my second-in-command bag!"

A menacing burst of laughter followed, and then a door slammed.

The Little Vampire clenched his fists. "Beasts!" he hissed, and disappeared to the front end of the hall, where the skittles must have been lying.

Leo the Gallant

Tony ducked down deeper into the shadow of the bush and watched the entrance to the pub nervously. It was not long before he saw George the Boisterous and Greg coming out of the darkened building. His heart was beating in fright, but the two of them had no interest in the surrounding area. Even though they had just ganged up together against Rudolph, they were now contradicting each other in loud and strident voices.

"Huh, that Leo of yours!" Greg exclaimed. "He could have made a mistake, you know."

"What do you mean?" George the Boisterous snorted. "I hope you're not daring to call my dear departed Leo a liar? Leo the Gallant – my childhood friend!"

"I didn't say that!" said Greg defensively. "But he might have misunderstood that bit about 'skittles' and 'whistles'!"

"Misunderstood?" George the Boisterous thundered. "If my childhood friend Leo the Gallant assured me that 'skittles' comes from 'whistles', then you can bet a clove of garlic that he was right!"

I'd rather not! Tony thought.

Greg cleared his throat. "But it wouldn't hurt just to try rolling the ball for once."

"What? You want me to betray the companion of my youth – Dracula give him peace! Not on your life!"

George the Boisterous rose indignantly into the air, and, snorting loudly, flew away.

"Stop, wait!" Greg called, soaring into the air after him.

In great relief, Tony watched as they grew smaller and smaller, until finally the night sky swallowed them up.

"George and his stupid Leo!" a husky voice suddenly said quite close to him.

Tony turned round with a start, but it was only the Little Vampire, who had crept up on him unnoticed.

"Next time, George will be rolling the ball as well. And then he'll be saying that's how Leo the Gallant told him to play, a hundred years ago," the Little Vampire grumbled. "When all the time, it was my idea to roll the ball."

"*Your* idea?" said Tony pointedly.

"Don't let's quarrel over details!" the Little Vampire retorted loftily. "Let's just celebrate my win!"

Tony pressed his lips together furiously, and kept silent. He had certainly not expected Rudolph to thank him. But now he was twisting the facts, and his behaviour was not a jot better than that of George the Boisterous.

Never Put Off Till Tomorrow

The Little Vampire may have felt that this time he had gone too far, because he resumed in a much friendlier voice, "If you like, I could celebrate my win by reading you a bit from the family chronicles."

"Would you do that?" said Tony. Such a tempting idea made him immediately forget how angry he had just been with the Little Vampire.

"'Course I will. What about tomorrow evening?"

"Not till tomorrow?"

"Have you forgotten that Aunt Dorothy is celebrating her Vampire Day tonight?"

"Oh yes —"

"You see, that's typical of me!" said the vampire roughly. "I'm always thinking of you, making sure nothing happens to you!" With that, he cast a sidelong glance at Tony's neck, and ran the tip of his tongue over his thin, almost bloodless lips. "I ought to go and fortify myself," he murmured. "I feel so peculiar . . ."

With a shudder Tony suddenly realized that the vampire could not have had anything to – ahem – eat yet. After all, the sun had just gone down when he had met up with him.

"Let's – let's fix it for tomorrow," he said hastily. "I

106

must go back to Dad now, too."

"So suddenly?" asked the vampire. "I thought you wanted me to read to you from the family chronicles."

"Dad's got a t-temperature," Tony stammered. "He might need me."

"Oh, really? What if I need you, does that count?" The vampire snorted. "Here you've been talking to me about true friendship and now, when you can prove it, you slink off."

"I – I really must go," Tony insisted. As always when they started talking about the vampire's eating habits, he had begun to feel very uneasy. "So we'll meet tomorrow?" he asked in a strained voice.

"Tomorrow, tomorrow," the vampire grumbled. " 'Never put off till tomorrow what you can do today.' That's an old vampire proverb." He paused. "All right then," he said at last. "Tomorrow, straight after sunset, at the ruins."

"Couldn't we meet somewhere else?" asked Tony hesitantly. He could not help thinking of Aunt Dorothy, and the fact that tomorrow she would be on the prowl once again . . .

"Where else?"

"On the road, for instance – where it turns right for Doombridge."

"That's fine by me," the vampire replied. "Now, let me through!" he added grumpily. "Otherwise I might forget that I'm Rudolph the Tenderhearted." He pushed roughly past Tony and stretched out his arms under his cloak.

Tony watched as he took off and even felt relieved to see him go. For a hungry vampire did not make a very pleasant companion, especially when that vampire held such a one-sided view of true friendship.

So Tony flew back to the Vale of Doom by himself and landed in front of Wolf's Hollow. After hiding the vampire cloak in a crack in the rocks, he crawled into the darkened cave. By the light of his torch, he checked that his father was still fast asleep, but noticed that his face glistened with sweat and looked rather pink.

But by now Tony was far too tired to give it further thought. He crept into his sleeping bag, switched off the torch and, straight away, fell asleep.

A Wet Blanket

When Tony woke up the next morning, sunlight was streaming in through the cave opening. He heard his father coughing outside in front of the cave, then the rustle of something that sounded like the pages of a newspaper being turned.

Tony got up and went outside. Dad was sitting on the grass. An open newspaper lay across his knees and nearby was a paper bag of fresh bread rolls.

Had he been into Doombridge already? It would seem so, because the bicycle was leaning against a different tree from the one last night.

"Hello, Dad!" Tony called. "Are you feeling better?"

Dad turned his head and smiled, though a little painfully. "Better?" he said. "No, actually, I'm not."

"But you've been off shopping, haven't you?"

"Yes, I thought there would be a chemist in Doombridge," his father replied. "The ointment in the first-aid pack hasn't done much good." And to demonstrate, he raised his right hand in the air.

Tony was shocked. The three fingers he had injured were now dark purple.

"Well?" he asked. "Did you find a chemist?"

"No. But I rang Mum. If the pain doesn't stop, she's going to come."

"What?" Tony exclaimed. "Mum's coming here?"

Dad tried to laugh. "I'd like to know what would happen if your fingers had been hurt like this. I bet you'd want to go straight home!"

"Home?" Tony gulped. "Do you mean you want to —"

"I don't want to," Dad replied. "Now don't stand there like a wet blanket! For the moment, we're still in the Vale of Doom. Let's have a think what we can do today, in spite of my injured hand."

But of course the possibilities were now very limited.

After breakfast – although "breakfast" was not quite the right word for it, for Tony's watch showed it was already half past twelve – they went down to the stream and tried a bit of fishing. But only one small fish took the bait, and Tony threw it back into the water.

Afterwards they sat in front of the cave and Tony read to his father out of his vampire book.

He read "A Smacking of Lips in the Grave", and as the story moved towards its climax and Tony's heart beat faster and faster, he saw his father stifling a yawn.

When Tony reached the part where the lid of the coffin had slowly opened and everyone standing around the grave could hear the horrible sound of smacking lips, he paused to prolong the excitement – and then noticed to his amazement that his father had fallen asleep.

"Don't you like this story?" he asked.

"Yes, sure, it's very funny," Dad answered sleepily. "Especially the bit when the children keep smacking their lips when they eat."

"The children?" said Tony in a puzzled voice. There were no children in the story. Obviously Dad had hardly taken in a word of it. Perhaps it had something to do with the pain killers he had just taken.

111

"I think I'll go and have a sleep, all the same," said Dad, getting to his feet. "You can tell me how it ends this evening."

"I will!" Tony nodded, and watched anxiously as his father disappeared into the cave. It might not be such a bad thing if Mum comes, he thought. Although, if it were up to him, she could leave it for another couple of days.

Guilty Feelings

As Tony had expected, his father did not ask how the story ended that evening. He simply rubbed some more ointment on his injured fingers and went to lie down once more.

As soon as Dad had fallen asleep, Tony crept outside. He closed the entrance to the cave behind him and looked around uneasily. The moon was shining, and, as if by a magnet, his gaze was drawn over to the tumbledown walls of the ruins which stood out sharply against the night sky. He wondered whether Aunt Dorothy was already out and about. He was certain she was, especially since she had had nothing to eat yesterday, her Vampire Day . . .

In any case, Tony was glad that tonight he could make a large loop to avoid going near the ruins.

He collected the vampire cloak from the cranny in the rocks and carefully brushed away the dust. As he did so, he wondered whether or not he dared fly.

After a little hesitation, he decided it would be better to go on foot. He felt safer on the ground, and the tall trees would shield him from being discovered. However, he did put the cloak over his shoulders – just in case! – and then he set off.

When Tony had walked through the little wood of fir trees, he noticed a small, dark figure detach itself from the shadow of the trees on the other side of the lane. He was about to call out a happy "Rudolph!" when it occurred to him that it might just as easily be Anna. With their black cloaks, pale faces, long, unkempt manes of hair, black stockings and canvas shoes, Anna and Rudolph were very difficult to tell apart from a distance. On the other hand, Anna had been wearing that hat with a veil, silk stockings and ankle boots when they last met. So it was quite likely that this was Rudolph . . .

Tony watched tensely as the figure slowly drew nearer until it came to a standstill just a few metres from him. Now Tony could see its small, snow-white face with its round little mouth and great, big, glowing eyes, and he could smell the heavy, sweet perfume of Fragrance of Eternal Love.

"Anna!" he said timidly.

"Hello, Tony," she answered in a distant voice quite unlike her normal tone.

The coolness of her greeting only strengthened his guilty feelings.

"You must be very angry with me," he began hesitantly.

"Yes, very angry!" she said.

"I – I'm very sorry about – about the coffin lid."

"What?" Anna exclaimed. "Aren't you sorry about anything else?"

"Of course. I'm sorry you had to spend all last night sitting by Aunt Dorothy's coffin."

She stared at him, her eyes flashing with rage. "That's not the only reason why I'm furious with you," she spat.

"What else have I done?" asked Tony in surprise.

"Huh! You've only come creeping into our vault and spied on me lying stiff and staring in my vampire sleep! As if I could help it!"

"But I didn't look in your coffin!" Tony protested. Suddenly he realized what must be worrying Anna: she presumed that he had seen her in her coffin looking cold and dead. And for Anna, who was going to so much trouble not to become a vampire, that must be worse than the punishment she had taken upon herself for his sake . . .

He knew he must be right, because she looked so startled at this.

"You didn't?" she said, blinking in disbelief. "You really didn't see me lying in that monstrosity of a coffin?"

"No! And I would never look in your coffin unless you had said I could first!" said Tony cunningly.

"Truly?" The glimmer of a smile flitted over her face. But she was still rather suspicious.

"Why did you look in my mother's coffin, then?" she demanded.

"Because there were only six big coffins, and not seven," he explained. "I wanted to see whose coffin was missing."

"Well, you made a big mistake coming into our vault in the daytime," said Anna reproachfully. "And then, to be so – so tired of life as not to shut the coffin lid properly . . ." She took a deep breath and blew it out. "If I hadn't said that I woke up and that it was me who pushed the coffin lid aside your life would no longer have been safe here in the Vale of Doom."

A shudder ran over Tony. "I know," he said wretchedly. "Rudolph told me."

"And Rudolph and I both got into terrible trouble!" she went on plaintively. "We might even have been sent away to live with relatives. We could have been sent to Australia!"

"To Australia? That would have been terrible – so far away! We would never have seen each other again," said Tony in dismay.

"Would you have minded if we hadn't been able to see each other ever again?" asked Anna, looking at him expectantly.

"Yes, of course," he said, feeling himself going red.

Anna blushed as well, and said in a gentle voice, "Just don't be so silly as to come into the vault in the daytime again. Then we'll be able to see each other a hundred times. No, a thousand times; no, a hundred thousand times more!"

Tony nodded, deeply relieved that Anna did not seem to be cross with him any more.

This Could Spell Trouble

"Now, come along," said Anna. "Rudolph's bound to be getting impatient by now."

"Rudolph?" Tony murmured. He had almost forgotten the Little Vampire during his conversation with Anna. "Where is he?"

"He said he would meet you in the chapel in the ruins. He's going to read something to you."

"Read something?" Tony felt his heart beating faster.

"I've absolutely no idea what he wants to read to you," Anna went on. "It's probably stories to do with this stupid Men's Club."

"I don't think so," Tony replied, biting his lip so as not to laugh.

"What do you mean?" Anna was surprised. "Do you know what he's going to read to you?"

"I . . ." Tony hesitated. Rudolph must have had a reason for not telling Anna which book he had in mind.

On the other hand, Anna had done so much for him that he did not want to keep any secrets from her.

"He promised he would read me part of your family chronicles," he explained.

"What? Part of the chronicles?" said Anna in a shocked voice. "Oh no, this could spell trouble!"

"Trouble?" Now Tony's voice was shaking. "Do you mean, for me?"

"For Rudolph, really," Anna answered. "You know, don't you, what happened when Aunt Dorothy found out that he had started to be friends with a – a human?"

Tony nodded. Rudolph had been banned from the vault, and in desperation had had to move into the basement of Tony's block of flats.

"Let's get a move on!" Anna urged. "So that we get to Rudolph before my grandmother, Sabina the Sinister, notices that the chronicles are missing!"

"But . . . I thought your family would have all flown off by now?" Tony asked, sounding puzzled.

"Let's hope so!" said Anna.

And with these words, she rose into the air and flew away so fast that Tony had difficulty in keeping up with her. She did not slow down until she had reached the entrance gate to the ruins, when she turned to Tony.

"Wait here!" she whispered.

She flew on further, and Tony landed near the gatehouse. He pressed himself tightly against the wall and waited, listening to the noises all around him. Now that he was alone, they sounded mysterious and a bit sinister. Even the light creak of a branch made him jump. When at last he saw Anna coming back, he felt as if he was being rescued.

"The vault's empty!" she announced in a whisper. "They're all off and away."

"Rudolph too?" asked Tony in dismay.

"No, he's sitting in the chapel reading the family chronicles – and all lit up as if for a party. It's unbelievable!"

"Lit up?"

"Yes, just imagine: he's got at least fifteen candles

alight. It's strictly forbidden to waste our precious candles like that. Just wait till I tell him what I think! Casually wandering off with our family chronicles, wasting all the candles . . ."

Anna snorted indignantly and shook her tiny fists.

"Come on, Tony, let's go!"

First, Secondly, Thirdly...and Fourthly

They flew around the tower and landed in front of an ancient building, its walls crumbling and entwined with plants. Bright light shone out through the small lattice windows.

"Is this the chapel?" Tony whispered, though the question was pointless because of the brightly lit windows.

"Yes," Anna replied, and marched up to the door with a grimly determined expression on her face.

"Wait!" Tony called.

"What is it?" asked Anna, stopping.

"I . . . er, the family chronicles, and that Rudolph was going to read to me from them . . ." Tony stopped.

"Yes?" She looked at him enquiringly.

"Don't tell Rudolph it was me who told you about it," he pleaded.

"Of course not!" she answered impatiently.

Then, with a violent movement that showed just how angry she was with Rudolph, she tore open the door and marched into the chapel. Tony followed her hesitantly, with a sense of foreboding. He could only hope there would not be a serious quarrel between the two of them.

But it seemed as though this hope was in vain. He had

hardly set foot in the chapel when he heard Anna's loud, reproachful voice.

"You thick-head! You idiot!" she raged. "I suppose you think you're the only one in this world? What if Aunt Dorothy finds you – we'll all be for it, you, me, and Tony too!"

Anxiously, Tony pressed himself into a dark corner near the door and waited, trembling, for the explosion. But, strangely, the Little Vampire did not so much as lift his head once throughout Anna's entire speech. He stayed sitting quietly at an old wooden lectern on which lay a thick volume – *The Chronicles of the Sackville-Bagg Family* – and acted as though he was reading with complete concentration.

The fact that he did not seem to care only made Anna more furious. "OK, pretend to be deaf – it won't help!" she cried in a rage. "You go and put the chronicles back in Grandmother's coffin this instant! But first, blow out all these candles – you wastrel!"

Still the Little Vampire did not move a muscle. He simply turned a page, unimpressed.

For a moment, Anna was speechless.

When she said nothing, for the first time Rudolph looked up from the book and asked in an unnaturally gentle voice, "Well? Have you finished?"

"Finished?" Anna gasped for air.

Before she could begin a new attack, Rudolph said in a dignified voice, "Now, just you listen to me a minute! Firstly, Grandmother has agreed to let me read the family chronicles. Secondly, Grandmother has agreed to let me read them here, in the chapel. Thirdly, Grandmother said I could light as many candles as I liked, because it would suit such a special occasion."

"Oh, well, please be so kind as to tell me what's so

special about the occasion?" asked Anna bitingly.

Rudolph grinned. "That I've now decided to become mature and sensible, like a grown-up vampire, and so I must be initiated into all the family secrets."

"Mature and sensible!" Anna sneered. "You need to do more than just read the family chronicles to become mature and sensible."

"You're just saying that because you're envious," said Rudolph calmly. "Envious because you can't read the chronicles properly by yourself yet."

"So what?" cried Anna, whose face had turned a dark red colour. "There are more important things to do! And I don't think it's particularly important to be like the grown-ups," she added. With that, she turned round and walked quickly past Tony to the door.

"Anna!" Tony piped, but Anna was so furious that she took not the slightest notice.

"And fourthly, Grandmother has forbidden anybody to disturb me while I'm studying the family chronicles," Rudolph called after her.

The door slammed shut with a bang, and Tony was alone with the Little Vampire.

Now Prick up Your Ears!

"I – I hope I'm not disturbing you," Tony stammered, walking hesitantly over to the lectern.

"You never disturb me!" the vampire replied. "At least – almost never. And in any case, not today," he went on in a patronizing voice. "As it happens, I've just found exactly the right story for you."

And when Tony stayed standing where he was in the middle of the chapel, the vampire commanded, "Sit down!"

"Sit down?" said Tony. Apart from the rickety chair that Rudolph was enthroned upon, there was nothing at all to sit down on – only a pile of rubble and rubbish on the floor.

"Well, stay standing then," the vampire answered with a giggle. "But don't keel over when I start reading to you from the family chronicles."

"I'd rather sit down," Tony murmured, and perched on a stone that was slightly less pointed and angular than the others. Then he waited impatiently for the Little Vampire to begin.

But Rudolph was taking his time. Like an actor before his main entrance, he tugged back his hair, rolled his eyes, blew out his cheeks, ran a hand over his cloak and

cleared his throat a number of times.

At last he began, in a pompous, lordly tone:

"*It was a dark and stormy night —*"

He broke off, and said in his normal voice, "I've set all this up rather well, haven't I?"

"What?" asked Tony.

"Well – all this family chronicle business. My grandmother, Sabina the Sinister, really does believe that I want to be 'mature and sensible'. Even Anna fell for it!" He rubbed his hands in delight. "You know, it was the only way to persuade Grandmother to let me look at the chronicles."

"Oh, I see," Tony murmured.

"As you can imagine, I've no intention of being mature and sensible – what's the point?" said the vampire with a giggle. "Now, prick up your ears!" he added. Then he took a deep breath, lowered his head over the book and began to read in a solemn voice:

"It was a dark and stormy night in the year 509 by vampire reckoning, when we had to say farewell to our dear vault, which had been a trusted and familiar home to us for so many years. Once more, we had to shoulder our coffins

and set out into a cold, unfriendly world.

"Ah, how can I describe the children's distress? Gregory was sobbing loudly. Anna's little eyes swollen with tears. Rudolph —"

Here the Little Vampire faltered, and coughed huskily a couple of times. Apparently he did not like to admit that he too had cried, so he simply left out the part that mentioned how distressed he had been.

"Oh, how good it is to have a family to share the burden of hard times!" he went on in a dignified voice. *"It was a night of care and trouble when six of us were forced to move the coffins into the ruins in the Vale of Doom.*

"As has been the practice of old in our family, there were two of us to each coffin. The arrangement this time was as follows: my humble self, Sabina the Sinister, with William; Frederick with Thelma; Dorothy with Rudolph. But – ah! – those two wreckers of the cemetery – my pen refuses to write their names – were not asleep either that fateful night! This is what happened on our third and last coffin shift.

"Sabina and William, Frederick and Thelma were already flying towards the Vale of Doom. Only Dorothy was still toiling down in the old well, desperately trying to free her coffin where it had stuck.

"Rudolph was at the edge of the well, helping Dorothy to pull up her coffin, when all at once he became aware of those creatures, McRook. and Sniv. – my pen is not able to write their names in full! They were approaching with the worst of all possible intentions, as was easy to see from their horrible wooden s—s and their loathsome, nauseating cloves of gar—. Rudolph was able to call out a warning to Dorothy. And then he seized on a heroic plan of action."

126

At this point, the Little Vampire paused and threw Tony a searching look. But Tony kept his thoughts to himself – for the time being, at least.

"Go on, read some more!" he said.

"All right!" the vampire growled, and he went on in a smarmy voice:

"While Dorothy waited, hidden in the well, Rudolph bounded out with a valiant leap in front of the two creatures, who immediately – my pen quivers at the very thought – tried to fall upon him. However, Rudolph took to his heels and ran straight towards the house of the unspeakable McRook—"

"Just a minute —" Tony tried to protest, but the Little Vampire cut in.

"No interruptions while I'm reading from the chronicles!" he hissed.

Then he went on:

"And so our brave Rudolph ran, closely followed by the two assassins. They were already rejoicing that they were about to catch him – when Rudolph rose into the air, flew on to the roof and climbed through an open window right into the house of the hateful McRook.

"Oh, how they ran! Up the path to the house, up the stairs to the bathroom door. But Rudolph had locked it from the inside, and now his greatest hour was approaching!

"He blocked up the plug and overflow holes in the bathtub and turned on the taps. He emptied nearly a whole bottle of bubble bath into it, and watched with a gleeful smile as the cloud of bubbles grew and the water rose.

"All this time, McRook. and Sniv. were hammering powerlessly on the door.

127

"Oh, how brave and valiant Rudolph was! He waited there, daring and unafraid, until the bath was overflowing and the whole room was filling with water. Only then did Rudolph leave the scene of his activities through the bathroom window, his work accomplished and – ah! – so well worth while.

"Our two arch-enemies were busy with their own problems for the rest of the night, thanks to Rudolph, and Dorothy was able to free her coffin in peace. Together with Rudolph, the Hero of the Night, she brought it safely to the Vale of Doom."

"The Hero of the Night!" Tony repeated cuttingly. "I don't seem to recognize you in all this. Talk about the crow dressing up as a peacock!"

"Peacock? Where?" said Rudolph, pretending to get excited and looking all around. "I can't see one!" he said with a grin.

"You know very well what I mean," said Tony severely. "I was the one who distracted McRookery and Sniveller from the coffin shift. I was the one who ran in front of them, luring them towards their house, so that Aunt Dorothy could pull her coffin out of the well."

"Oh, I see!" said the vampire in amusement. "And now I suppose you want all the credit given to you in our family chronicles?"

Tony gulped. "Give . . . *me* . . . the credit in your family chronicles?"

"Hey, you've gone as white as a sheet!" The vampire giggled.

"I . . ." Tony's hands suddenly felt as cold as ice. "I don't want to be mentioned in your family chronicles," he begged.

"You see!" The vampire rolled about with laughter. "I

knew that, so I told my grandmother, Sabina the Sinister, the whole story as if it had happened to me. I only did it for your sake – out of true friendship! You do understand, don't you?"

"Y-yes!" Tony stammered.

"There you are!" said the vampire with a grin. "That's just the way I am – Rudolph, your true friend!"

Till I Die

Suddenly, in a quite different, demanding voice, Rudolph added, "Now, swear!"

"Swear?"

"Yes. That you won't speak of the chronicles to anyone."

"Not even to Anna?"

"Anna?" The vampire gave a broad grin. "Yes, you may talk about the chronicles to her. After all, she is one of the family. Now, swear it!" he added impatiently. "I haven't got all night."

"How – how do you want me to swear?" asked Tony anxiously.

"Simple!" the vampire answered, and closed the chronicles with such a bang that a cloud of dust rose from the book. "You lay your hand on the book, and then you say after me . . ."

"What do I say?"

"Don't ask so many questions! Just put your hand on the book."

Slowly, Tony got up from his uncomfortable seat. He walked over to the lectern and stretched out a trembling right hand.

"Not your right hand!" said the vampire grumpily.

"The left one – the one that comes from your heart!"

Tony hesitated. Should he really lay his hand on the chronicles – especially his left one, since, as Rudolph said, it did come from his heart – and swear? Was there not a danger that if he did he might turn into a vampire himself? He felt an icy shudder. As if from miles away, he became aware of Rudolph's menacing laughter.

"Hey, you look as if you've swallowed a goldfish!" he cackled.

"N-n-nothing will happen to me?" asked Tony anxiously.

"What on earth might happen to you?" the vampire enquired.

"I . . . afterwards, I couldn't . . ."

"What?"

"Afterwards, I won't become a member of your – family, will I?" Tony asked haltingly.

"It's not as simple as that!" the vampire retorted. "And anyway, you have to want to yourself."

"But I don't want to!" Tony cried, more forcefully than he had actually meant to.

"Steady on, steady!" the vampire soothed him. "Now come on, my stomach is rumbling!"

Still trembling, Tony laid his left hand on the heavy book. As he touched the well-worn gold cover, a strange warmth seemed to stream through his fingers . . .

He drew back – then pulled himself together and once more laid his hand on the dusty old book.

"Ready?" asked the vampire, who at the same time had risen to his feet.

Tony nodded. His heart was in his mouth.

"Well, then – pay attention!" said the vampire.

> "By this book do I swear now
> To guard its secrets till I die.
> And should I ever break this vow
> May Dracula's rage upon me lie."

There was suddenly a lump in Tony's throat. He gulped, and in a husky voice began to repeat the oath.

> " 'By this book do I swear now
> To guard its secrets, yes, I'll try . . .' "

He stopped. The leather binding under his hand suddenly felt very hot.

"What is it?" asked the vampire. "You've only said half the oath! And anyway, it goes 'till I die'."

" 'And should I ever break this vow'," Tony went on

in a husky voice, " 'May Dracula's rage upon me lie.' "

"Just so!" said the vampire with a cackle of laughter.

Then he pulled the chronicles from under Tony's hand with a jerk and clamped the book firmly under his arm.

"Let's go," he said, in a gravelly voice.

Rudolph the Poet

"You – you're not going to read any more?" asked Tony in disappointment, casting an anxious look at his left hand. His palm was burning, but there was no red mark to be seen.

"No," the vampire answered curtly and began to blow out the candles.

"What about your story?" Tony cried. "You promised to read it to me today."

"Did I promise that?" said the vampire with a conceited, self-satisfied smile. He was obviously flattered by Tony's curiosity.

"Yes, you did! And you haven't told me anything about the chronicles, either. What the year 509 by vampire reckoning means, for instance."

The Little Vampire grinned.

"If there's something you can do today . . .
It'll be better done tomorrow, that's what I say!"

he proclaimed in a mysterious voice. Then he blew out the last candle.

All at once, it was pitch dark in the chapel.

"Quickly now, off we go!" the vampire hissed, and Tony heard him going to the door. He groped his way uncertainly behind Rudolph, and was heartily relieved to reach the outside without falling over anything.

The Little Vampire was waiting for him, hopping from one foot to the other impatiently.

"You'll find your way home alone, won't you?" he asked.

"Y-yes," said Tony, surprised at the vampire's sudden politeness.

"All right, then," said Rudolph and turned to go.

"J-just a moment!" said Tony.

"What is it now?" the vampire growled.

"I . . . " Tony cleared his throat. "Will we see each other tomorrow?"

"You can hardly wait to find out what happens, can you?" The vampire giggled. "All right, then! Come to the chapel tomorrow evening – I'll be there."

With these words, he turned and hurried away to the main part of the ruins. Tony waited till Rudolph disappeared through the dark doorway. Then he set off for the cave. He went on foot and kept cautiously to the shadow of the trees.

But there was nothing suspicious to see or hear, and Tony reached Wolf 's Hollow without mishap. After he had listened for a moment, and no sound reached him from the cave, he carefully pushed the rucksacks to one side and crept into the darkness.

Now he could hear the soft, even breathing of his father and he dared to switch on his torch. Dad was lying there, peacefully asleep.

Relieved, Tony blocked off the entrance to the cave, climbed into his sleeping bag and switched off the torch. But this time, he did not fall asleep straight away. The evening had been so exciting . . . He saw Anna in his mind's eye as clearly as if she were in a film . . . how angry she had been with him at first, then how they had made it up . . . and Rudolph, sitting there at the ancient wooden lectern, reading from the family chronicles . . . and then that oath . . .

Softly, Tony recited it once more:

> " 'By this book do I swear now
> To guard its secrets till I die.
> And should I ever break this vow
> May Dracula's rage upon me lie.' "

It did not actually sound like a genuine old vampire oath, he thought – more like one of Rudolph's poems.

But it could be genuine. After Tony had said it through once more, he suddenly realized that the burning sensation in his hand was not so strong any more . . . In fact, the burning feeling had completely disappeared, and his left hand felt quite normal.

With a deep sigh, Tony fell asleep.

Follow the spine-tingling adventures of Tony and his vampire friends in the next book in this chilling series:

The Little Vampire in Despair